LAST PRIEST STANDING

And Other Stories

by

Richard Infante

The Lambing Press
Pittsburgh
MMXV

LAST PRIEST STANDING
And Other Stories

For my mother and my sisters.

Contents

Foreword by Mike Aquilina............................1

The Waters of Tribulation................................9

Birdland...55

Saints and Sojourners...................................102

Promise...220

Fields of Grace...249

True Colors...286

Last Priest Standing......................................319

FOREWORD

By Mike Aquilina

Pity the man who must introduce a work of fiction. The authors do make it hard for us. We approach our task with the words of Mark Twain before us: "Persons attempting to find a motive in this narrative will be prosecuted; persons attempting to find a moral in it will be banished; persons attempting to find a plot in it will be shot."

What then are we to do? Denied the freedom to explore motives, morals, and plots, some fall to praising the author—and maybe that's the secret hope behind Mr. Twain's restrictions. But I know the author of this book too well to praise him overmuch. He finds flattery even more painful than the speculation of overexcited critics.

One does what one can, and I can talk about these stories because I know them well. To me, they're not literary artifacts. They're memories. The first time I encountered Richard Infante's fiction, he was in a coffee shop in Pittsburgh reading aloud from "The Waters of Tribulation." A jazz pianist accompanied him, tracking the drama rather perfectly, I'd say. I felt caught up in the scenes, caught up in the floodwaters myself, and I remember each episode as if I'd really been part of it. When much later I read the story in print, my mind retrieved small details as if from an event rather than a story.

That's to the author's credit. I am by nature a distracted reader and by circumstance too busy. But these stories are something more than realist. They're real. And so they hit a reader—at least this one—not the way words usually do, but rather the way life does.

This is all the more remarkable because the life Richard Infante describes is, in many ways, alien to me. I am, like the author, a Catholic. But he is a priest, while I'm a layman, and most of his protagonists are priests. Indeed, many of his secondary characters are priests.

To the non-Catholic reader, this may seem a distinction without a difference; but the difference is rather profound. We believe that ordination changes a man more surely and deeply than immersion in fire. Theologians speak of an *ontological* change, a change in *being*, that configures a man to Jesus Christ in a unique and permanent way.

We don't just assent to this belief. We experience it. Priests are not better than we are, but they are different from us. Even the anticlerical French speak of the clergy almost as if they're another species or another sex. But those categories don't quite apply to the priests who populate Richard Infante's stories. They're unmistakably male, and they're all too human. Yet they have the difference, and it's the special gift of this author to let us see it from the inside. He manages to reveal something of the mystery without sacrificing any of the mystique.

This makes the stories fascinating to Catholics, of course, and some of them appeared first in Catholic literary journals. But there is nothing parochial about them. The vocation of a priest is different from my own, but his vocational struggles are similar to mine in many ways—and they illuminate my own, even by their differences. James Joyce said: "If I can get to the heart of Dublin, I can get to the heart of every city in the world. In the particular is contained the universal." Getting to the heart of priesthood, Richard Infante gets to the heart of vocation, and commitment, and the possibility of communion between God and man.

It is good to invoke Joyce here because he was, like Infante, a Catholic in the realist tradition—"steeled," as the Irishman put it, "in the school of old Aquinas."

For Aquinas, for Joyce, and for Infante, that "school" is realist, but the term seems to beg a qualifier. For the realism of a Catholic artist is not a gross reductionism or mere naturalism. Nor is it reactionary, like magical realism.

We might call it sacramental realism. What these characters do is a sacrament—an outward sign—of who they are. Joyce referred to his character's happenstance disclosures as "epiphanies," "little errors and gestures—mere straws in the wind—by which people betrayed the very things they were most careful to conceal."

In creating art this way, the writer of fiction is imitating God. We may call the technique "realist" because it is true to the world God created, where human creatures are free and bear the consequences of their choices.

A Catholic artist strives simply to see what's there—and it does tend to involve motives, morals, and plot (*pace*, Mr. Twain). The world follows a design, which makes plot possible; and the design implies a designer, an author. Saint Augustine said that God writes the world the way human authors write words.

Like the author of a short story, God discloses himself through his creative actions.

The world is charged with his grandeur. It is sacramental, with signs everywhere, evident to the priest and to the artist, though in different ways.

No one should be surprised, then, to find that a sacramental quality pervades these stories. It's there in the way characters reveal themselves. But it's also there, as it is in the world, in the way rivers move and mountains stand. Wherever water flows, it's a sign of divine power, creative and destructive. It's a sign of baptismal life. It's an image of the Holy Spirit.

The stories are sacramental also because of their subject matter. They deal with the sacraments of the Church. The drama moves forward by way of Baptism, Confession, Communion, Confirmation, Orders, Anointing, and Matrimony. It is surely no accident that the book contains exactly seven stories, as the Church has exactly seven sacraments.

But these statements have brought me perilously close to banishment, if not gunshot, and so I will cede the remaining pages to Father Richard Infante, who has stories to tell us —stories so real that they become events, saving events.

THE WATERS OF
TRIBULATION

"Where you goin'?" Phil asked, threading his fishing rod through the random thicket.

"Just up here a ways. C'mon," John, the younger one, said and kept stomping through the tall, wet brush. "There's a way down to that pool on the other side of that big stump up there."

"We shoulda got a boat and went up Twin Lakes," Phil said, pushing aside the branches of a thornberry bush snapping back at him in John's wake.

They had been fishing together the past couple years since that first spring in the seminary. But Phil had never worked this stretch of Patch water, as the locals called the little stream running by the fifty houses and mobile homes that made up the Patch. They could hear the stream babbling and tried to hush their clumsy steps along the sodden bank.

"Is that Elmer? John, is that Elmer?" Phil pointed to an old house across the gravel road where a man and a young woman seemed to be arguing; they could hear the strained pitch of their voices but not many words.

"Hunh?"

Phil pointed to the rickety frame house, again. The woman's arms waved wildly on the porch. They watched as the man threw his hands down in disgust and turned away from her.

"That *is* Elmer," John said. "That's his car."

They both stood quietly for a while in the tall weeds along the bank of the creek, each waiting for the other to say something. The car sped away and the woman stormed into the house, the screen door banging shut behind her.

"Who's the woman?" John asked.

"Doesn't his sister live around here?" Phil asked.

"Maybe that was his little sister," John said. "The one with the kids."

"Hope so," Phil said and turned down the bank toward the creek.

"Hope he ain't fishing without a license," John said and chuckled with the veiled reference to their celibate life that the seminarians often teased about.

"I got my license last week," Phil said, only half hearing the younger man and missing the joke altogether.

So the two men spent their morning in the dark, swirling currents of the Patch creek, knee high in the swift, muddy waters. John, in his mid-twenties, worked the stream more vigorously while Philip, in his early thirties, seemed content to let his bait do most of the work. They fished in silence for a couple hours without so much as a bite, losing worms more than catching fish in the fast, swollen stream until the gray southwestern Pennsylvania sky showered yet another deluge of cold, spring rain.

By the time they scrambled back to the car, they were soaking wet. They threw their gear in the trunk. The rain pounded on the car as it splashed along the asphalt roads.

When they got back to St. Vincent's, the rain had slowed to a drizzle. A few hooded monks and the tall, stately rector were crossing the parking lot after noon prayer.

"There's the man," John said, motioning toward the rector. "He'll be archabbot someday."

"He'll be bishop," Phil said.

They took their hip boots off and splashed toward Leander Hall, their residence the past few years. They sat on the top step of the huge porch, under the Roman arches, looking out across the pond and the wet fields to the mountain ridge at the horizon.

"You two get skunked again?" Elmer slapped his friends on their backs with his heavy hands. "Glad I wasn't counting on trout for lunch."

"The water was too fast and muddy," Phil said.

"It's been raining too much lately," John said. "The stream's too high."

"Ah-hunh," Elmer said with an exaggerated nod of his head. He sat down between them. "Sure, sure it was."

"Wise guy," John said and winked at Phil. "All you caught was an earful this morning."

"What?" Elmer asked.

"We saw you down there in the Patch bottoms," John said with that mischievous grin. "You and some woman were squabbling on the porch."

"That's my baby sister, you knuckleheads," Elmer said. His face grew ashen and sober.

"Ah-hunh," John mocked him.

"Sure, sure it was," Phil teased.

"I'm worried sick about her," Elmer said.

"What's wrong, Elm?" Phil asked, his tone concerned and drawn now.

"Ah, it's the guy she married." Elmer shook his head. "I never liked him from the get go. Thinks he's better than us because he's from the city—kinda like you, Phil."

"Thanks, Elm," Phil said and rolled his dark eyes.

John muffled his laughter. "There's no guile in that Israelite."

"He left her for good and she's stuck renting that big old house in the Patch with the kids."

Elmer's broad face grew more grave. "I've been trying to fix a few things for her here and there —like this morning, I was puttying around the kitchen windows where the water's been leaking through."

Phil and John sat listening to their friend's lament.

"So I told her she should think about moving back with our mother and brother on the farm and she hit the roof," Elmer continued. The more he talked, the more his thick hands waved out in front of him and his voice became shrill with exasperation. "Mom's been watching the kids in the daytime anyhow while Noel's at work. She could save some money if she lived at home but she keeps thinking Mr. Wonderful is coming back. He ain't coming back. He was cheatin' on her even before they were married."

"Sounds like she's got some problems," Phil said.

"That ain't the half of it," Elmer went on, his voice more discouraged with each breath, his head sagging lower and lower. "She's just a kid—like you, Johnny—twenty-three. She's got two children, she works all day, no husband to take care of her and the youngsters. She was always the smart one in the family, my folks' favorite—mine, too. Then she went off and married the first good-lookin' guy that paid some attention to her. I told her to wait awhile, but nobody in the family listens to me, anyhow. They all think I'm wasting my life going back to the seminary after a dozen years."

"Well, you are, but that's beside the point," John teased and drew a friendly swat on the shoulder by Elmer.

"Would you look at that," Phil said in a distracted mutter.

The three men stopped their talking and just watched the colors form out of the moist April air over the empty field a couple hundred yards away. They could see where the colors slowly bowed in an arc rising up above the ridge line, the spectrum of red, orange, yellow, green, blue, and purple bands sharpening in brightness with every passing moment.

"Look at that!" John said in amazement.

The perfect rainbow congealed in a shimmering brilliance under the bright spring sun and then turned down toward the field in an array of colors that dazzled the men. After a few minutes it began to disappear as miraculously as it had first appeared.

"I've never seen a rainbow form like that right in front of my eyes," Phil said.

"You lived in Pittsburgh all your life, what do you expect?" John said. "Now it's starting to evaporate—check it out, Elm."

As the rainbow dissipated in the subaqueous sky of the heavy April day, Elmer's eyes filled with tears. With Noel on his mind, the promise and beauty and fragility of it all made his middle-aged heart ache with care. He got up and hurried into Leander Hall.

A couple days later, after noon Mass and lunch, Elmer, Phil, John and the other third-year seminarians were in their scripture class with Fr. Benedict Bonn, O.S.B., a distinguished scholar of national reputation. While Fr. Benedict lectured on the fifth chapter of St. John's gospel, Elmer sat slumped in his chair, looking out the window at the steady rains pelting the garden beds. He was brooding about his sister, the farm, his leaving the seminary that first time to do mining, the trouble his family had ever since their father died: his cross.

"While there is some confusion over the name of the pool, Bethesda in Hebrew," Fr. Benedict continued in his clear and strong voice at the lectern, "scholars generally agree that it was distinct from the spring of Siloam which is mentioned in the ninth chapter. In fact, archeological excavations this century have unearthed a pool in Jerusalem with five porticoes."

Across the aisle, John caught Phil's eye with a little nod of his head, and then gestured for him to look at Elmer, who sat in the desk chair directly in front of him, motionless and seemingly disinterested in everything save the rain.

"The Dead Sea scrolls at Qumran also refer to a certain pool near the temple known as the *Bethesdatayin*," Fr. Benedict explained.

John began to push Elmer's chair leg carefully and slowly with his foot, while Elmer sat oblivious and immobile. Phil put his hand to his head and bent down over his notes to hide his amusement from their professor.

"The confusion between the two pools," Fr. Benedict went on, "arises from the fact that at Siloam there was a spring which, during the rainy season, gushed water throughout the day. This could have been mistaken for the stirring of the pool of Bethesda, since to both were attributed powers to heal the ill, the blind, the lame, and the crippled."

John eventually succeeded in angling Elmer's chair slightly toward the window, accentuating his misdirection, while a few of the other seminarians began to notice Elmer's distraction.

"This stirring or troubling of the waters was believed to be caused by an angel of the Lord." Fr. Benedict noticed the men's furtive glances and moved toward Elmer, who was still peering out the window. He leaned over him in his ominous black habit. "Rise, take up your pen, and wake up," he said to Elmer, who was startled to attention by the monk's close voice, as well as his classmates' suppressed laughter. 'Trying to figure out how Hezekiah dug the curved tunnel from both ends at once, are you Elmer?" Fr. Benedict teased. Everyone was laughing now.

"Hunh?" Elmer managed to say as his face flushed with embarrassment.

"The stonecutters used the echo of their comrades' voices to guide their labor in the tunnel. The Hebrew inscription from 700 B.C. describing this amazing engineering feat is still legible today," Fr. Benedict continued teasing him. He checked his watch and then turned to the class. "That's enough for this afternoon."

As the seminarians hurried out of the room, laughing, Fr. Benedict called out across the huddle of bodies in a low, commanding voice: "John, I'd like to see you a minute, please."

A few hours later, John and Phil were in the small chapel to join the other seminarians for evening prayer. They were all dressed in their clerical shirts and black pants. Elmer came in late, in the middle of the opening hymn, and made a quick sign of the cross before he sat down. By the time he arranged the ribbons in his breviary, the singing was over and the fifty or so men settled down to pray. In a moment, Elmer was caught up in the rhythm of the rolling voices praying the psalms, in a recitation born of habit as much as devotion:

"If the Lord had not been on our side, this is Israel's song..." one side said and completed the strophe before yielding to the other group of seminarians across the chapel:

> *Then would the waters have engulfed us,*
> *the torrent gone over us;*
> *Over our head would have swept*
> *the raging waters...*

The seminarians prayed in alternation through the psalm to its completion. In the peace and serenity of those familiar, fraternal voices, Elmer's eyes welled up again and he was lost in thoughts about his sister's troubles, about how she had distanced herself from him ever since he had decided to reenter the seminary a few years ago. *She makes me feel like I've abandoned the family*, he thought, though he knew he had given the better part of a dozen years of his life to keep their small farm going after their father died, and waited until his younger brother knew enough to take over. *I practically raised her after Pop died*, he thought. *I tried my best.*

Then he heard the rector's deep, resonant voice intone the familiar blessing that concluded their prayer, and it drew him out of his anxieties for a moment. The seminarians shuffled out of the chapel, but Elmer just slumped down, heavy and still in the hard wooden chair, and stared intently at the tabernacle housing his Lord.

Later, at supper in their dining hall, John spoke quietly to Phil at the salad bar. Outside, the heavy rains pounded the wet garden.

"Did you see Elmer?" John asked.

"No. I think that stuff with his sister got him down," Phil said. "He looks upset."

Another seminarian approached the two of them at the salad bar. "Think it'll rain?"

"If it gets any worse, we better start building an ark," Phil said.

"It's rained for twelve days straight," John said and scooped some beets into his bowl. Phil nodded to John toward the back and the two of them headed for a far table.

The dining hall was filled with about four dozen seminarians and a few of the Benedictine monks that taught them. The warm laughter of the young men and their joking across the tables gave the dimly lit room an almost palpable conviviality that seemed to hover over the dozen tables like soft turns of light glimmering with each rising voice. After finishing their meal, John and Phil hurried out of the pleasant camaraderie of the dining hall and up the stairs in search of Elmer.

But they could not find Elmer that night. They checked a few places around the seminary and then went to the campus ministry office where Elmer worked with the college students. The two girls in the office hadn't seen him that night either.

"I'll betcha he's down his sister's," Phil said.

"Probably," John said. "We can't bother him there."

"Maybe he's down the gristmill," Phil said.

"He goes there once in a while and helps Brother David grind some flour," John said. "It's worth a shot."

So the two of them gathered a few beers from Phil's refrigerator and got into John's Jeep, which was parked behind Leander Hall. They drove to the mill, though it was only a couple minutes away, because the incessant spring rains drenched the earth that night as they had for the past two weeks. They parked in front of the gristmill in the rough gravel lot. When they got inside they set the beers down and shook the rain from their clothing and hair.

Then they started laughing at the sight of Brother David scampering around with a large pail to catch the steady drops of rain plopping down through the high ceiling.

"Well, don't just stand there! Get one of those buckets and put it under there," Brother David said, pointing to another steady drip splashing off the old floorboards.

In a few minutes, the three of them had positioned several pails beneath the major leaks.

"Thanks," Brother David, a burly man of thirty with a full, red beard, said with a nod.

"Here," Phil said and handed him a can of Rolling Rock.

John snapped his can open, too. "Was Elmer around tonight?"

"No, I didn't see him," Brother David said. "Something wrong?"

"He's got family problems," Phil said and took a long swallow of beer.

"Who doesn't?" the monk said.

Sitting on the gristmill floor, the three of them talked and drank and talked some more about the guys who had left the past couple years, about the women they had married and their first kids. The steady plop-plop of the dozen or so buckets catching the leaks echoed through the mill. Eventually, the conversation came back around to Elmer.

"He's all worried about his sister and her kids," John said.

"You shouldn't have to worry about a pretty woman like that," Brother David said.

"You have to worry about them the most," Phil said.

They whiled away another hour drinking and telling stories about Phil's years on the Pittsburgh fire department and John's spelunking exploits in the Laurel Caverns.

"When it rains, it pours," Brother David said.

"I feel like Noah before the flood," Phil said looking around at the cavernous, creaking old building.

"Jonah in the belly of the whale," John said and caught a drop of rain in an empty beer can that rang with a piercing *ping*. The men quieted at the sound, as if it signaled the end of the night, the end of the beer.

Ping-ping. The rain tapped on Elmer's window. *Ping.* He bolted upright out of bed and stared into the blackness of his unlit seminary room. He was coming out of a terrifying nightmare into a dreamy consciousness of dread and fear. He woke up gasping for air. He knew something was wrong, desperately wrong, but he could not gather his thoughts; his heart pounded in his deep chest. He felt a raw ache in his body that augured trouble. It was the same feeling he had that night his father died and he had driven two dreadful hours through the winter's cold only to get to the hospital too late to say goodbye. He shuffled to the window of his third-floor room and peered out into the watery blackness of the April night.

"Noel," he whispered against the relentless rain. "Oh, God, help her and the kids." He glanced at his digital clock, the numbers glowing green and menacing in the dark: 2:33 AM.

He turned on the desk light and quickly dialed his sister's phone number—nothing: her line was dead.

He dressed in a frenzy, banging drawers and throwing hangers around the room. He grabbed his coat and keys and hurried out the door. Halfway down the hall, he stopped at his friend's door and knocked on it several times.

"Who is it?" John's thick, angry voice barked at the door.

"John, I need help—please," Elmer pleaded. "Get Phil, hurry—it's Noel and the kids—I think the Patch is flooded out, please! I'll meet you at my car." John got out of bed but his head was slow and heavy from the beers. He went out into the dark hall, but Elmer was already bounding down the stairs.

Outside, Elmer frantically rummaged through his trunk driven by that confusion of fraternal and paternal care that always welled up in him in regards to his little sister: flashlights, blankets—"No rope," he muttered under the shower of rain clanging on the car roofs.

"I got rope," John said as he came up beside him.

"Get it, please, John," Elmer said.

"What's going on?" Phil said as he joined his friends, his jacket yanked over his dull, aching head in a futile attempt to keep it dry.

"Elmer's worried about his sister and her kids down the Patch. He thinks they might be flooded out," John said. John continued to search in the back of his Jeep until he found the ropes he used for caving. "Got 'em, Elm, c'mon. We'll take the Jeep in case the road's washed out."

Elmer grabbed his flashlight and handed the blankets to Phil. As they pulled out of the seminary parking lot into the hostile night, Phil looked back at Leander Hall and saw a few lights flick on as they sped away. The floodlights of John's Jeep pushed some brightness through the thick shower of rain pounding off the road before them.

Elmer sat in the front seat, hunched over, muttering his dread: "Her phone's dead—please, no."

John put the radio on the weatherband station. Almost immediately, the voice confirmed their worst fears: "...hazardous flooding in

31

many streams and rivers in Allegheny, Westmoreland, Washington, Greene and Fayette counties..." followed by the accompanying list of flooded streams which included the Patch Creek.

"Jesus, no, please," Elmer prayed under his breath.

"Maybe they've already been taken out," Phil said.

And for a moment, Elmer's broad face lit up with the possibility of a rescue that he had not foreseen. "Maybe."

"Hold on!" John slammed on the brakes but the Jeep splashed and slid in the muddy waters washing up over the swollen stream and across the road. By the time they stopped sliding, water covered halfway up the tires.

"We can't go any farther," John said with an exhalation of his tensed breath.

"There's another way into the Patch," Elmer said. "Past the old Tyler Hotel and down Crawford road."

"You mean where that old stone tunnel is?" John said.

"Yeah, that's it," Elmer said. "C'mon, let's go."

John sent the Jeep splashing through the foot-high waters and back onto the main highway. They drove for a few minutes more in the torrent but to Elmer it seemed like hours. A silence settled on the young men as they began to realize what they were facing. The rain drummed mercilessly on the car.

"I hope the tunnel's not flooded," Phil said and then wished he hadn't, almost as if saying it might make it more likely.

"Slow down around the bend up here," Elmer said to John. "Park it on the rise."

The three of them jumped out of the Jeep with thick swirls of rope, blankets wrapped in plastic, and a couple flashlights and splashed down the road toward the tunnel. When they got close enough, Elmer gasped in horror. "God, no!" The black, swirling waters seemed to fill the mouth of the tunnel. The three of them stopped dead in the cold, rushing waters, ankle deep where they stood.

"We can't climb over it; it's too slick, too steep," John yelled against the raging rain and waters. For a moment, they stood silent and defeated, the threatening waters swirling all around them and encroaching on the frail, barren trees.

"Look again," Phil shouted as he squinted through the blur of rain and water, shadow and stone. "The water's only halfway up."

"We can make it," John said.

"There's a railing along the one side and the walkway's raised a foot or so above the road level," Elmer said with determination. "C'mon."

The three men splashed across the road to the hillside and used the thin trees along the shoulder to steady their steps through the cold creek waters.

"How long is it, Elm?" John asked and tied the rope around his waist.

"About fifty or sixty feet. It curves in the middle there," Elmer said. "That's the low point, too. Be careful, John."

"Phil, tie this around the pole there and wait here until I come back," John said. "Gimme ten minutes."

With some deep, rapid breaths, John descended into the swirling, lightless cavern and in a few moments was belly deep in the watery chaos. He held the railing with both hands and labored with each step against the flooding current. A length of rope slipped from his shoulder with each unsteady step.

"Lord Jesus Christ, have mercy on me, a sinner," he muttered. His prayer sounded small in the dark din of the turbulent tunnel. The rushing water was rising. He could barely hear Elmer's faint voice calling out his name with encouragement. The black water was at his shoulders when he reached the low bend in the tunnel; his breaths came quick and hard. He had to go under. He had been in dozens of watery caves before but they were shallow and he never had to go under and hope to come up on the other side.

"Lord Jesus Christ, have mercy on me, a sinner," he prayed to choke down his terror. He drew one, last, deep breath, closed his eyes, and he was under, holding on to the rickety iron railing for all his worth. He could feel the strong current push at his legs, so he crouched along the railing and pulled his way deeper into the abyss. He fought back the panic of death in that watery tomb and scrambled with all his strength along the railing. He tried to keep count of the seconds. *Our Father, who art in Heaven*, he thought. *Help me.*

After a few more seconds, he raised himself carefully and reached his hand up through the waters. Then the tortuous moments were over and his head bobbed up above the swirling water line. He gulped the air. "Thank you," he said with his head and shoulders above the stream.

John continued to struggle against the tugging current until, at last, he was on the other side and the water was around his knees. He untied the rope from his waist, stretched and knotted it around the heavy iron post at the end of the railing. He stopped to catch his breath momentarily; he had to go back to get Elmer and Phil. He thought of the desperate young woman he saw on the porch yesterday and her children at the mercy of the flooded stream and, in a moment, descended back into the furious maelstrom.

When he came up again out of the low point in the tunnel, John thought he heard Elmer's voice calling out his name, but the rush of water spilling through the tunnel drowned out any clear sounds. He clenched his hands on the railing and in a few moments he was clear to the chest and could hear his friends' voices echoing his name into the tunnel. He called back excitedly: "It's okay—we can make it! We can make it, Elmer!"

Elmer's strong hand reached out for John and pulled him the last few steps out of the tunnel.

"You okay?" Phil asked him.

"Yeah," John sucked the wet air down as quickly as he could.

"You have to go under—you got to crouch down—pull yourself along," John said between breaths. "You got to hold on tight—the current's pretty strong—cold, too."

"C'mon, let's go," Elmer said.

"Just a minute," John said. "It's not too high on the other side, maybe two, three feet. They should be okay in the house, Elm. Phil, tighten the line around the pole and fix the flashlight to your belt."

They waited a few minutes in the rain and floodwaters until John was ready.

"Okay, let's go," John said with a nod. "Hold onto the railing and use the rope to steady yourself. Leave the blankets."

Without another word, the three of them entered the swirling black hole, staying close. When they got to the low point at the middle of the curved tunnel, the water splashed at their necks.

"It took me about thirty seconds to crawl along here under water," John explained. "Elmer, count a minute, fill your lungs, and c'mon through—we don't want to get caught down there together."

With a deep breath, John went under and disappeared in the murky blackness. Elmer counted to sixty, said a short prayer, and he was under, too. Phil hesitated a moment, distracted by some fluorescent graffiti scrawled on the tunnel wall in a kind of jagged, gang hieroglyphics. Under the dull beam of his flashlight, the only cryptic shapes or words he could recognize was something that looked like a bird pierced through by a sword or cross. Then he gulped air and followed his friends.

On the other side, John found Elmer's hand reaching up out of the current and he pulled him free. In another minute, the two of them were helping Phil up and out of the deeper water. He came up coughing. Then, the three of them worked their way along the rope and railing to the mouth of the tunnel where the water splashed at their thighs. Stopping to catch their breath and to survey the Patch in front of them, they were exhilarated with the possibilities of life.

"C'mon," Elmer said. "They're just over there a ways."

"Secure your line around that pole, Phil, and we can use it to get back," John said. "Watch your step as we make our way across—there's a lot of stuff floating in that mess."

Elmer took the secured rope from Phil, threw it on his shoulder and sloshed across the flooded Patch like some water buffalo on a charge. John and Phil were right behind him fording the flooded stream. A large tree limb bobbed menacingly by them in the black rushing water.

"No-el! No-el!" Elmer yelled into the rainy night. "No-el!" Her house was the fifth one from the tunnel. In a few minutes they saw the porch. Elmer held his flashlight up and started waving it at the house.

"No-el! No-el!" he yelled above the droning, merciless waters. He thought he saw a candle light flickering in the second floor window. In another couple minutes, he was on the steps and tied the line around the porch post. The water was more than a foot deep on the first floor. As he shone the light into the front room, he saw his sister coming down the stairs with the little boy in her arms and the girl close beside her.

"Elmer! Elmer!" she cried out to him.

"It's okay. It's okay," he answered. "We're here."

He met her on the stairs and they hugged while the children clung to them with all their strength. "Jessica, you're safe now," Elmer said and smoothed his rough hand over her little head. "Billy, you okay?"

"C'mon! C'mon! This is no time for a family reunion," Phil said when he came into the room and flashed his light on the four of them holding close at the foot of the stairs. "We got to go now; the water's rising."

"How are we going to do this?" John said to Phil, looking toward the children and Noel.

"We'll put them on our backs," Phil said. "You kids ever ride horsey back?"

"Ah-hunh," little Billy said, his frightened eyes brightening for an instant.

"Okay, honey," Noel soothed her boy. "You ride horsey back with Uncle Elmer's friend here. C'mon dear, let go, now."

"His name's Phil, Billy." Elmer coaxed the boy.

The little boy reluctantly let his mother loose and clung round Phil's neck with all his strength. John moved near the landing where Elmer hoisted Jessica onto his back. "This is John, Jessie; he's my friend," Elmer said. "He'll take good care of you. Don't be afraid."

"Okay sis', climb on," Elmer said. The brother and sister looked at each other for a moment and, in that glance, they were transported back more than a dozen years to the time after their father died—when she would wait for her big brother to come home from the mine and he'd give her a ride on his back around the front yard, like their father had always done.

"Thank you, Elmer," she said through her tears and climbed onto his back. "Thank you for coming for us."

In a few moments, the three pairs of them were outside in the rain, the men holding onto the rope that stretched across the roiling water, the children and their mother holding onto the men with all their might. The three men were afraid to say what they all dreaded with the rapidly rising flood waters; there was no turning back.

"C'mon," John urged as he grabbed a flashlight and took the lead into the cold muddy waters. "Walk slow and steady—don't go too fast. We're with the current now."

Though the rain had let up some, the waters were rising swiftly as they moved carefully along their lifeline. The extra weight on their backs helped the men secure their steps in the perilous, waist-high waters. The little boy was sobbing for his mother but Phil reassured him to keep a tight grip around his neck. They all sensed how close they were to death, even the little ones.

"We'll make it, Noel," Elmer whispered up to his sister as they strained through the turbulent water. "We'll make it."

When John neared the mouth of the tunnel, he got nauseous and almost fell with dread. The swelling waters nearly enveloped the opening of the tunnel. They could never get through there with the children.

"What's wrong?" Elmer yelled over the splashing flood. "Don't stop!"

"We can't make it," John said, wanting not to frighten the children, though he could feel Jessica trembling on his back. "We can't make it."

The greasy odor of fear seemed to encircle all of them as they stopped, hopeless and terrified, before the flooded tunnel.

"No! God, no!" Elmer spat out his frustration.

"Is that all you can do?" Noel chided her brother. "Did you bring my babies out here to drown!" the young mother said to her brother in that sarcastic tone of voice his family used to berate Elmer and fix him in the failure they thought was his right by birth.

But he just stood there, not answering her taunt, in the middle of the turbulent waters swirling all around him. He hung his head in recognition of his folly, taking her venom into his heart and poisoning his limbs stiff and lifeless. And it seemed the weight of his whole, burdensome life was on him now, sinking him deeper into that black pool of rising water: family, vocation, farm, mine, failure. He seemed to accept this watery death as his due after thirty-eight years, and the fact that he had led them all, friends and family, into this fateful trap, crushed him with an iron doom. And then, something lifted out from within him like a groan, or a sigh, barely audible:

"If the Lord had not been on our side,"
    this is Israel's song...
Then would the waters have engulfed us,
    the torrent gone over us;
Over our head would have swept
    the raging waters."

"What?" Noel screamed in his ear. "What did you say?"

He did not answer her harsh voice but paused calm and confident in the midst of their dilemma. He was undaunted, now, filled with hope and resolution.

"C'mon," Elmer directed. "We have to go back to the house." He turned his exhausted body and started to wade across the rising water, holding onto the rope. His friends followed him; there was nothing else to do. "Hold the light up, Noel."

The unsteady troop followed Elmer and began to slowly make their way against the current which now came up to the legs of the three riding on the men's backs. Then the rope went limp and they saw a long piece of porch railing tumbling in the current and their line going with it. "Leave go," Elmer said. "Leave go of the rope."

"I can't make it," Phil said. "My legs are cramping—grab the boy," he moaned.

John reached forward for the slipping child and Elmer stretched back to grab a fistful of Phil's jacket and keep him up.

Not here, Lord, Elmer prayed. *Not here.*

They stood helpless and beaten in the middle of the raging waters, afraid to move, paralyzed with dread, the children sobbing, their lives dangling by a thread.

Elmer was the first to hear the distant muffled voices straining above the splashing stream. Then he saw the dim light sweeping over the watery death in rhythmic turns. "Help! Help!" he yelled at the top of his lungs. "Over here! Over here! There's a boat—it's coming this way! Wave that thing, Noel!"

And they were shouting for help in unison now, and waving the only flashlight that still worked. It was like a dream come true; the little motorboat puttering closer to them across the dangerous waters. "Help! Help!" they called out; the children, too. Within a few moments the boat was near them and dropped a heavy anchor. The two men in long yellow slickers and hats helped the children and their mother into the safety of the boat.

"I don't think we can get you guys in without capsizing," the one man said to Elmer, John and Phil. "Can you hold on and we'll pull you across to the shallower side? Stay clear of the propeller."

The three exhausted men leaned over onto the sides of the boat. Elmer smiled at his sister and her children huddled in their dry yet fragile safety. One of the men looped some ropes under the seminarians' arms and around their backs to secure them to the craft, their legs still submerged in the creek waters.

"Go! Let's go," he said to his partner and the flimsy boat puttered its slow and saving way across the flooded Patch to the high ground by the main road, where a crowd of people were waiting as they disembarked.

Elmer, dazed and exhausted, found himself being attended by a few seminarians putting coffee to his lips, wrapping blankets around him, asking questions that he was too tired to answer. Everyone seemed to be flitting about, moving faster than his eyes could focus. He couldn't hear much, either, for the hum of exhaustion droning in his ears. Then he saw him or rather the silhouette of him, like in a dream: the tall stately bearing, his hooded head illumined by the alternating flash of yellow and orange lights coming from the emergency vehicles on the road: an angelic figure, still and serene, detached from the bustle of people tending to Elmer and the others, almost floating beyond the din.

"You okay, Elmer?" he asked, his limpid, tranquil blue eyes now a breath away from Elmer's face.

"Yes, Father," Elmer said and his eyes closed involuntarily. His head jerked up with the remnant of trouble still alive in his mind. "Phil! Philip! Where's Phil and Billy?"

"They're fine, Elmer. Everyone's safe," the rector said in that resonant voice of his that let Elmer drift off to sleep, secure as a baby lulled to rest in his mother's arms. "You did a great thing, a courageous thing, tonight. The Lord is with you."

The next thing Elmer remembered, he was waking in a rattling van or something, the piercing siren calling him to consciousness. "Noel! Noel!"

"We're here, Elm," his sister whispered. "Your friends are in the other one."

"Thank God, we made it," Elmer said and reached a limp hand over to touch the heads of his niece and nephew.

"I'm sorry I said those things back there," Noel said. "You're a great brother. You're going to be a great priest, too."

"I hope so," he said. "I hope so."

Noel took his hand from her drowsy son's head and pressed it to her face. "I'm sorry, sorry for everything, Elmer."

"God love you, girl," was all he could manage to get out at that tender moment, before the ache of his body gave way to the welcome sleep that overcame him as they rode to the hospital in the rattling ambulance.

It was dawn when the rector returned from Latrobe Hospital, secure in the knowledge that John and Phil, Elmer, his sister and her children were resting in warm beds. He would call their families to let them know their loved ones were safe. He was proud of the three men's courageous actions and of how the other seminarians had banded together to help them in the middle of the night. He rested against the pillar of the Roman arch on the Leander porch and lingered awhile, a tall and graceful figure. He looked out across the thick primordial mist blanketing the pond and fields to the horizon. A morning hawk sailed on a current of air and seemed to hover in flight above the bare fields. The dawn sun was peeking over the Laurel Ridge and it lit up the underbelly of clouds with patches of yellow-orange light sparkling along the billows of blue and white. The mist and mountains, the hawk and light, the fallow fields, seemed to him full of promise. He gazed awhile as the brilliant sun rose white and dazzling over the horizon; the mist lifting slowly and beginning to dissipate beneath the warm April light. He imagined Jesus rising from the dead on just such a morning and he was filled with joy for his life's work, hope for the future of the Church. He thanked God for their deliverance and the tears came like consolation.

BIRDLAND

"How can you listen to that noise?" Aunt Sophie said.

"I can't anymore." Fr. Joseph Sadowski turned off the radio on the fading jazz saxophone. "We're beyond the signal now."

After the last pit stop near Interstate 80, they had been driving north along the freeway without so much as a headwind to encumber their drive. *At this rate we'll be in Erie in no time*, he thought as they passed a camper with some children pressing their faces against the side windows. His senile uncle droning in the front seat seemed to be enjoying the ride, the bright, summer sunlight sparkling through the windshield and illuminating the dashboard before him. Fr. Joseph Sadowski was driving fast in his burgundy Thunderbird as was his habit the past few years, ever since he was appointed the bishop's Secretary for Family Life with its dizzying blur of board meetings, ceremonial banquets, conference speeches, parish Masses, and ecumenical events that took him from one end of the diocese to the other, crisscrossing counties, usually late.

"Is he drooling again, Joseph?" his aunt asked, taking tissues from her purse and handing them to him between the gray bucket seats. "Here, wipe his face."

Fr. Joe, as the children called him, reached back for the tissues and dabbed at the spittle running down his uncle's chin and onto his white shirt.

"Walter's like a child anymore," Aunt Sophie muttered. "Do you think we can stop soon, Joseph, in case he has to go?"

"We'll stop in Meadville," he said, pressing the gas pedal, not wanting to lose time. "It's just a few minutes up the road." He had grown accustomed to acquiescing to his godmother's requests over the past few years. Since his mother's death, he often spent holiday meals with his godparents; they had no children and adopted their godson, a forty-five year old priest, as if he were an orphan. And with the deepening familial bond, he also inherited this duty of driving his aunt and uncle to the family reunion every August between the Solemnity of the Assumption and the Queenship of Mary, at the old family farm in North East, a few miles outside of Erie. It was a vestige from the old country, where the faithful from all over Poland made the annual pilgrimage to the Shrine of Our Lady of Czestochowa in homage to the icon of the Black Madonna, at the Pauline monastery atop Jasna Gora, the Bright Mountain.

As they sped up Interstate 79, passing through the Conneaut Swamp, Aunt Sophie prattled on about a nephew's new job or an aunt's illness, about a cousin's upcoming wedding and newborn babies, trying to bring her godson up to speed about the recent news of their extended family. But Fr. Joseph was only half-listening. With each passing mile taking them beyond the diocese, he was beginning to unwind, his mind relaxing from his priestly concerns. He was glad to be out of his black clerical clothes, happy to be with his family, far from the tensions that had been swirling around the chancery since the pedophilia scandal had broken in Boston. At most parishes he visited for the past few months, he had been met with angry questions from discouraged Catholics. He let out a deep sigh for the heinous crimes committed by his fellow priests against innocent children. Looking to the heavens, Fr. Joe caught sight of a flock of black terns in the pale blue sky, swirling above the watery habitat, wheeling one way and then another, banking sharply in unison, their lighter gray wings flashing in the brilliant midday sun, as they made their descent to the sprawling bog below. He followed their graceful course until he lost sight of the whirling flock swooping down behind a stand of trees that rose above the murky swamp.

Something about the birds' twirling flight toward the hidden refuge brought to mind the wet, windy night he was called to the hospital last week.

"She's in here, Father," the nurse had said, and led Fr. Joseph past the nurses' station to one of the rooms, pulling back the curtain for them to enter.

"I'm Fr. Joseph," he said to the weeping woman he took to be the young woman's mother, and to her friend.

The mother, a hand to her face, could only point to her daughter lying in the hospital bed, with tubes and lines attached to her mouth and arms, her thin chest, swelling slightly, rhythmically, in time with the puff of air echoing from the ventilator.

He put his priest's stole around his neck, the violet side showing, to anoint her, and placed the bottle of holy water on the table nearby. He took the oil stock from his shirt pocket and twisted off the lid. "Her name?" he asked.

"Michelle Marie," her mother whispered.

Then Fr. Joseph looked closely at her bloated, white face. *Oh, my God,* he thought. *It's her.* He held his breath for a few seconds.

"Father?" The nurse nudged his arm.

"I know her," he muttered without looking at Mrs. DeSanto. "I know your daughter, Michelle. We spoke a few times this summer." Pieces of their conversations began to rise in his mind as he fumbled with his rites book. He recalled her fearful premonition of death just a month ago in his office. *She was only twenty-five,* he thought. *How could she have known?* "She said she was never baptized; is that right?"

Her mother nodded, her eyes wincing with dread.

Fr. Joseph set his oil stock aside and reached for the holy water. He took the cap off. Then he turned his stole to the white side for the baptism.

"Michelle Marie, I baptize you in the name of the Father..." as the priest poured water over the crown of her head he heard her mother's low moan "...and of the Son..." he doused her again "...and of the Holy Spirit. Amen." A third time he bathed her head in the waters of mercy. He brushed the trickle of water from her brow onto her red hair with his fingertips.

"My baby, my baby," her mother whispered and leaned against the other woman. When he placed his hand on Mrs. DeSanto's shoulder, Fr. Joseph felt her body trembling.

"Thank you, Father," the nurse said. "Thanks for coming."

He recalled sitting in the waiting room for a few minutes, replaying Michelle's desperate, rambling discourse as she searched for God in their summer's dialogue. Then he ventured out into the rainy night, the wind pushing the water into his face, soaking his black clothing, as he splashed across the parking lot to his car.

As they drove over some rumble strips in the highway, the tires hummed loudly in concert with Uncle Walter's droning, waking Fr. Joe from his reverie in time to slow the car down and veer onto the Erie exit ramp for

Route 5 toward Northeast with his aunt still talking in the back seat.

Glimpsing the great lake, Fr. Joseph saw the light gleaming at the horizon, the sky bright and blue with puffs of white clouds floating over the dark green waters.

"We're in Erie, Walter," Aunt Sophie said. "Just a few minutes, now."

Fr. Joseph glanced to the north, again, but was unable to see the lake through the buildings and trees that lined the state road. He twirled the radio dial until he heard a newscaster announcing the lakefront weather: "Fair and mild for the weekend, winds five to ten miles per hour; a high of eighty-three on Sunday."

Fr. Joseph enjoyed this stretch of the drive along East Lake Road, the local name for Route 5, through the town of Harborcreek, past the Benedictine sisters' monastery, and into the acres of vineyards along the lakefront to the farm. He didn't know whether it was the people or the place that drew him more, the family reunion or the land itself, but he knew that this annual pilgrimage gave his priestly life a kind of temporal rootedness, a sense of belonging to a clan or tribe whose origin in this continent was born on these lakeshores. He needed that. His life had become fragmented and disparate working in the chancery these past few years, not rhythmic as in parish life, but moving in an uneasy syncopation: before this but after that, not here nor there, between now and then, straddling time and place like some wayward sailor tossed on the endless tides of next to never: drifting from one event to the next, never in a place long enough to lay anchor. He turned onto Cemetery Road in the midst of the lush August vineyards. His godfather was droning, again, in the seat beside him. "We're here," Aunt Sophie said and patted her husband's shoulder. Fr.

Joseph rolled the window down and took a breath of the lakefront air, hoping for a trace of the late summer vintage, but that fragrance was still a couple of weeks away.

In a few minutes, they were slowing down onto the long driveway of the Sadowski family farm, the gravel crunching under the tires of his Thunderbird. The sprawling, white farmhouse stood out in the midst of the neat rows of grapevines that surrounded their old property, now only a few remnant acres. Fr. Joe saw a killdeer, a pair of black bands across her white breast, hobble across the driveway, dragging her brown wings, instinctively trying to divert his approaching car from her nestlings hidden in the grass. Fr. Joseph slowed his car to avoid the beautiful decoying bird, which took to flight with its piercing call echoing above the vineyards. Cars were parked every which way, scores of people milling about the dozen picnic tables and the brick grill by the lone apple tree beyond the small vegetable garden, the rising smoke lingering in the limbs and then dissipating like an apparition of angels ascending to the heavens. Aunt Sophie fussed in her purse and Uncle Walter began to rock slightly in his seat as Fr. Joseph parked the car alongside a row of others.

When they saw Fr. Joseph get out of the car, some of the children ran up to meet him, squealing and chattering. One of the little girls jumped into his arms. He could not remember her name at first, though he knew she belonged to his cousin, Janice, because of the family resemblance: the fair skin and light freckles, the blond hair in a ponytail, her wide-set blue eyes, and that broad, toothy smile just like her mother's.

He stared at her face for a moment before her name came to mind. "Hiya, Monica."

"Bobby said a bad word, Father Joe," the little girl said and held his face in her small hands.

"I didn't mean it, honest," the older boy said, poking his cousin's leg as she hung suspended in the priest's embrace. "It just slipped out when we were talking about where Grandpap went after he died."

"Joseph, could you give me a hand with Walter, please?" his godmother said, standing alongside the car on the passenger's side. "The ground's bumpy; he might fall."

"Sure, Aunt Soph," Fr. Joseph said. Setting the little girl down, he spoke to her loud enough for the other children to hear. "He's in heaven, honey, with God. Your grandpap's in heaven."

He made his way through the gaggle of children, patting some of their heads as he moved past them. He led his godfather across the gravel driveway and toward the picnic tables.

"Sit him here, Joey," his Aunt Stella said and made room for them at the closest table in the large yard. "You got here at the right time, Sophie; we're almost ready to eat, dear—er, Father Joey."

Some of their relatives, mostly women, came over to greet them as they took their places at the table. Fr. Joseph and Aunt Sophie helped Walter get seated. When his arms were free, his aunts and cousins hugged and kissed the priest. Other women were bringing large platters of food out from the kitchen, the plates clacking as they set them down on the various tables to feed the nearly seventy hungry Sadowskis. Fr. Joseph exchanged hugs and pleasantries with his aunts and cousins, enjoying the familial commotion enveloping them. Then he made his way toward the grill where the men gathered around the fire and meats. He passed the keg of beer standing in a plastic tub of ice emblazoned with a red maple leaf.

"Joseph, about time you got here," his Uncle Stanley said. "Good to see you, young man."

"Good to see ya, Unc," Fr. Joseph said and shook his hand firmly, reestablishing their bond of familial blood. After the young Joseph's father died, Stanley, the eldest brother, had taken him under his wing. Fr. Joe enjoyed the chorus of greetings, the hand-shakes and slaps on the back from the men, and the chance to forget that he was a father, too, for a while.

As soon as he saw his cousin, William, cook-ing at the grill, Fr. Joe remembered that time as boys that they almost drowned in the Lake, when a sudden storm capsized their flimsy fish-ing boat before they could get back to shore. "Hey, Billy," Joseph said. "Since when do they trust you near the fire?"

The men, who had been drinking through the afternoon, laughed at the priest's teasing of his cousin; they all knew they were as close as brothers.

"Joey, you want to go fishing after supper?" William teased him back as he placed the sizzling kielbasa, barbecued chicken and fresh perch onto the large white platters held by some of the other men. "We'll take the boat out."

"Never mind," Fr. Joseph said, cognizant of his relatives enjoying their repartee. "Ever since you almost got us drowned, I don't go out into the deep water anymore."

"We can anchor offshore." William slid some hamburgers and pork chops off of the grill and onto the platters, waving his free hand at the thick, aromatic smoke billowing from the grill like incense "If we don't catch anything, you can preach to the gulls. At least they'll listen to you."

The score of men laughed heartily at the cousins' verbal duel, especially with the priest participating in the parrying.

"Ah, enough now, you two," another uncle said and finished a last swallow of his Labatt's. "Your aunts will get upset if we're having too much fun."

The men, beers in hand, moved to join their families at the picnic tables, some bringing the last of the smoking fish and meat with them, others filling pitchers of beer.

The familial din quieted as they settled at the dozen picnic tables. Uncle Stanley asked Fr. Joseph to offer the blessing. Some women were still bustling between the kitchen and the tables with horseradish and other condiments. Fr. Joe began with the sign of the cross as a few stray teenagers joined their families.

"Heavenly Father," he intoned in his sonorous voice, looking out on the pleasant faces of his extended family, many with the characteristic broad face and fair skin of the Sadowskis, the straw-blond hair and watery blue eyes. He prayed a simple thanksgiving to

God. Then Fr. Joe gestured a cross over the picnic tables: "...and may Almighty God bless our family table in the name of the Father, and of the Son, and of the Holy Spirit. Amen." On cue, the rhythm of pleasant voices and the sound of serving utensils clinking off the platters began to echo over their assembly in the midst of the vineyards. Sunlight glinted off the metal and glass on the tables. Above the gathering, soft brown mourning doves cooed from their perch on the telephone lines; a small flock of dark starlings nestled in the apple tree with the dissipation of the smoke, an occasional rasping note emanating from the hungry birds. Fr. Joe enjoyed the sizzling kielbasa and Erie perch, as bowls of coleslaw and platters of pierogi were passed across the tables. The meal was delicious, and everyone ate heartily. Even the few babies in highchairs at the end of the tables gulped down spoonfuls of homemade applesauce from their mothers. Large, cold pitchers of iced tea, lemonade, water, and beer were drunk quickly in the warm August air. Fr. Joe had a second helping of his Aunt Stella's haluski, the cabbage and onions sautéed to a slight crisp, the rich butter evident in every mouthful of tender noodles. Joseph forgot himself in the safe, familial gathering, the meal and camaraderie insulating him from the pressures of the priesthood and chancery politics he left behind in Pittsburgh. He enjoyed a couple of glasses of Labatt's with his meal. Several white gulls had begun making sweeping arcs lower over the vineyard, hovering for an opportunity to feed; a few more perched on the rooftop. A dozen of the women and their daughters brought out a variety of pies and cakes, cookies, and nut rolls, with steaming thermoses of coffee. This last course of the meal was more animated with the serious business of eating concluded; some of the teenagers began to drift away from the tables. Fr. Joe no-

ticed several of the children gathered around
the concrete birdbath near the apple tree, feeding the starlings small pieces of homemade
bread that they had smuggled from the table.
He watched the white gulls swoop in, trying to
bully the smaller, feisty starlings with their
bold size. He recalled being a child himself,
thrilled with the feeding of birds.

"Did you have enough to eat, Joey?" his
Aunt Sophie asked as she wiped a paper napkin
across Walter's mouth.

"Too much." Fr. Joe patted his stomach.

"Sophie, don't you think Joseph looks like
Pope John Paul?" his Aunt Stella said as she
poured him another cup of coffee. "When the
Pope was still young and strong?"

"Yeah, like a family resemblance or something," Aunt Helen said. "Your mother's people were from Wadowice, you know."

"If he's related to the Pope, I'm becoming Protestant," William said. His wife, Marian, slapped his arm playfully.

"Dad, when can we go to Birdland?" Teddy asked his father. "You promised."

"Tomorrow, we'll go tomorrow." William poured himself another glass of beer. "After Mass. Maybe Uncle Joe will come with us."

"Birdland?" Fr. Joe said.

"The waterfowl preserve on Presque Isle," Marian explained. "It's what the kids call it, Joseph. We took them in the spring and they've been talking about it all summer."

"Sure, I'd enjoy going with you guys, Bill," Fr. Joe said.

"We'll all go tomorrow," Marian said, reassuring her children.

Fr. Joe was lost, now, as he had hoped, lost in a kind of aural ambiance like he became while listening to an intricate piano solo from his modest jazz collection. Amidst the clearing

75

of the tables, the squawking of the children playing in the yard, the familiar conversation with his aunts and uncles, his cousins and their children, Pittsburgh seemed a world away, his diocesan duties set aside, for a time, forgotten in the matrix of this familial reunion: seventy saints and sinners feasting in the promising August vineyards. His harried mind was decompressing, releasing the tensions of priestly service and ecclesial scandal that had consumed him for months. And while he talked and teased at table, he noticed a pair of hawks gliding on the currents of the air, swirling high above the vineyards. He felt like he was in flight, too, free and drifting on the course of the conversation moving about the yard, deflecting questions about the bishop's prospects for elevation in the Church, losing himself in the welcomed play and patter of his extended family under the soft, diffused light of the lakefront at dusk.

"So, Father Joe, whaddaya make outta that church scan'al in Bos'on?" His cousin's skinny husband, Daryl, who had drunk too much beer, asked as he approached the table.

Fr. Joseph bowed his head, the tension rising up his back and neck. He was thankful that most of his relatives hadn't heard Daryl's slurred question. The priest was grateful, too, when his Uncle John tactfully deflected his son-in-law's awkward remark. Fr. Joe rose from his bench without haste, muttering something about "taking a walk," anxious to get away from the discordant moment that had strained the otherwise pleasant talk at table.

"Hey, wait up, Joe," his cousin, William, said. He hurried to catch up with him. "Don't mind him; he can't hold his liquor," William said, condemning their cousin's husband with an accusation that was akin to mortal sin among the Sadowski men.

The two of them walked beyond the family property, through the vineyards, and across the highway. They stopped when they reached the hundred stairs that descended to the beach. They peered out across the fifty miles of the great lake trying to glimpse the coast of Canada in the fading August light, like they had done innumerable times when they were teenagers, searching into mysteries more than discovering answers.

"Can you see it?" Fr. Joe said.

"No, I can't," William said. "Not enough light."

They stood awhile, together, peering toward the horizon, watching a lone plane make its deliberate way toward the airport on the other side of Erie.

"I missed him again," Fr. Joe said.

"Who?" William asked.

"The Pope!" the priest said. "He was in Toronto last month for World Youth Day and

I couldn't get away. You remember the story about Uncle Walter chauffeuring the Archbishop of Krakow around Pittsburgh for a week during his visit thirty-five years ago?"

"Kind of," his cousin said.

"I was supposed to meet them but I was at the Pirates game and it went into extra innings and by the time I caught the bus back to Polish Hill they were already gone," he said. "Who could've guessed that Archbishop Karol Wojtyla would become the Pope?"

"Right place, wrong time," William quipped, his memory refreshed with the story that was part of their family's lore.

For a while more they watched the pulsing, green lake and the luminous, purple sky, without saying much, waiting intuitively for the calm to settle upon them under the failing August light. After a few minutes, they returned to the reunion.

Marian was waiting for them with the porch light on when Fr. Joe and William got back to the farmhouse. Children were still playing in the evening yard, trying to catch the flickering fireflies in the dusk.

"Everything okay?" Marian whispered to her husband as they embraced.

"Yeah, it's okay," William said and kissed her cheek.

"I'll get you a couple of beers." She motioned to the men to have a seat on the porch.

As the dusk light faded, the extended family began to shift toward their places for the day's end: the teenagers meandering along the periphery of the yard, the older folks moving from the porch to the rooms inside with the sleeping babies, the locals to their cars for the short ride home, some women leading the smaller children upstairs to the attic of bunk beds, a group of men with beers gathering around the kitchen table with a deck of cards, some young adults lingering on the other side of the deep porch, with Fr. Joe on the Amish rocker and William and Marian on the swing, talking about their teenage summers boating and fishing, swimming in the Erie moonlight and warming themselves near a driftwood fire. Within an hour of nightfall, the farmhouse was still and mostly quiet save for the half-dozen men playing poker in the kitchen and the dozen or so teenagers trying to live beyond the limits of the day, their complicit laughter on the porch an attempt to hold back the inevitability of the closing darkness.

With an occasional nighthawk fluttering past the porch, Fr. Joseph fell asleep in the rocker with the whispering voices of the flock of teenagers audible from the other side of the large porch that wrapped around the farmhouse. William and Marian slipped into the house; they could see that he was exhausted. "Let's go swimming in the lake, tomorrow," were the last words that echoed in Fr. Joe's ears as he drifted off to a deep, restful sleep, his large head hanging over the back of the rocker, his heavy breaths exhaling up and out into the still August air, his deep snore like some rattling percussion drumming in an obscure yet rhythmic improvisation. Then it became more like droning than drumming, a rumbling of the waters pushing up and bursting the taut, dark skin of the lake in a rush of white froth that flapped out of the roiling water: a thousand, glistening white doves winging into the bright, blue sky, water dripping from their feathers in the intense sunlight and Michelle, in her white gown, wet and rising amidst them into the enfolding mantle of the Madonna of Czestochowa that wrapped them, dove and woman alike, in the blue embrace of the heavens. Fr. Joe awoke momentarily from the breathtaking dream, exhaling heavily into the night. He glimpsed hundreds of bright stars speckling the night sky over Lake Erie and then rocked himself back to sleep, wrapped in the warm blanket that Marian had draped over him.

With the first soft lake light of Sunday, Fr. Joseph awoke to the dawn chirping of the sparrows and wrens feeding in the yard on the crumbs from yesterday's feast. He got up slowly and set the blue blanket over the back of the rocking chair. As he stretched, all he remembered of his fading dream was the wild, white winging of birds.

He was among the first to use the men's shower; the hot water soothed his aching back and legs. He changed his clothes and got a cup of black coffee in the kitchen. He found his cousin, William, swaying slightly on the porch swing.

"You up, already, Billy?" Fr. Joe sat near him on the Amish rocking chair with the broad armrests that had been his bed.

"I didn't sleep much," William said, sipping his coffee.

"Maybe you ate too much," Fr. Joe said. "Me too."

"Yeah," William said. "I should've drank more. But I watch it around the kids."

"How late did you guys stay up playing cards?" Fr. Joe sipped his black coffee.

"Well past midnight," William said. "Maybe one or so. You were out by then."

"Who won?"

"Who do you think?" William said. "Uncle Carl—he always wins."

The two cousins went on talking in the cool morning light about whatever came to mind: Marian and the kids, their teenage summers on the lake, William's work with a new engineering firm in Cleveland, the Pirates' new ball park that Fr. Joe had already been to that season, the miserable atmosphere in the diocese because of the pedophilia scandal in Boston, until everything was cleared away and Fr. Joe could say the thing that had been on his mind since he left Pittsburgh.

"I buried a young woman on Tuesday," he began. "I only knew her for a few weeks. I met her at the soup kitchen. She had a hard life."

The screen door banged shut behind Marian. She joined William on the swing, holding her hot cup of coffee.

"I buried a young woman last week," Fr. Joe started, again. "She had curly red hair; she was frail and light as a feather. She was insistent about getting baptized. She said she was afraid of dying without knowing God."

"Did you baptize her, Joe?" William asked.

"Well, that's the thing." Fr. Joseph set his tepid coffee down on the floorboards next to his rocking chair. "I persuaded her to sign up for the RCIA group that was forming in September. I gave her some things to read, but she still had that fear in her eyes the last time I spoke with her."

Marian held her hand up to the side of her face to deflect the morning sunlight. "So, what happened?"

"About a week ago, we were on call and I got a call from Mercy to go and anoint somebody in the middle of the night." Fr. Joseph's eyes misted momentarily. "It was her."

Marian sighed. William took a last swallow of coffee.

"It was an aneurysm; she was in a coma," Fr. Joe pleaded his case. "Her mother was there with a friend. I knew she had expressed a clear and ardent desire to be baptized into Jesus Christ. I had the holy water so I baptized her right there on life support. Mrs. DeSanto told me her full name: Michelle Marie."

Distracted by the cawing of an unseen crow, they all glanced toward the vineyard.

"I went back to St. Mary's but couldn't get to sleep," Fr. Joe continued. "I kept wondering how she knew—like she had a premonition or something. On Sunday we got a call that she had died."

"You think she went to heaven, hunh?" William said, anticipating the point of his cousin's story.

"She never regained consciousness," Fr. Joseph said. "She couldn't sin. Her baptism was heartfelt; I knew it."

"You mean she went right from your hands to God's?" Marian whispered.

They were startled when a pot or pan clanged on the kitchen floor. Others were rising, too.

"I better go and wake up the kids." Marian touched William's hand and went into the house.

Fr. Joe grimaced. "There's more, Bill, but don't tell your wife."

William leaned a little forward on the swing.

"She was abused in high school. I think that's what set her off on drugs, petty theft, the street life. It was a priest; he was a few years ahead of me in the seminary. He's gone now." Fr. Joseph paused, his head down as he rocked a few times. "I felt like it was my responsibility to get her to God, Bill."

"And you did," William said. "You tried to make up for what he did to her."

The men became quiet for a while, the oblique silence a way of acknowledging the mystery of it all. Then, a few children came bounding out of the house and into the yard, causing the sparrows and wrens to take flight.

"Bill, help me set up the altar for Mass," Fr. Joseph said.

The two men moved one of the picnic tables a little forward of the porch steps.

"I'll get the icon," William said.

Fr. Joseph walked to his car to get the vessels and gifts, the books and vestments, for Mass. As he neared his car, he saw a flock of Canada geese, about thirty, or so, standing in the Sadowski field, majestic and orderly like a parliament, preening and ruffling their brown wings, looking in the stubble for something to eat, their long black necks rising gracefully from their feathered bodies. Fr. Joe stopped for a moment when he noticed the sentinel goose looking directly at him. Then, a couple of vehicles, full of his relatives who lived in Erie, pulled in and parked near his car. They helped him carry his things for Mass as they walked to the farmhouse together.

The tantalizing aroma of coffee drifted through the kitchen windows and rose into the morning air. People started milling about, exchanging greetings as they took their places at the tables and benches. Dozens of sparrows and wrens gathered in the apple tree. The flock of starlings perched on the fence rails and vineyards, instinctively looking for another meal. The mourning doves, in pairs, settled higher on the telephone lines, their plaintive cooing echoing above the low murmur of voices in the yard. A few gulls swooped above the vineyards in graceful arcs.

The image of the Black Madonna hung from the porch post behind the makeshift altar, the mother in blue regal raiment, the child bejeweled in orange, angels about their majestic crowns atop their serene dark faces. The older Sadowskis were familiar with the traditional hagiography that purported that the original icon was painted by St. Luke on planks of wood from the table of the Holy Family.

And so, Fr. Joseph Sadowski began the Sunday Mass for the family reunion, deep in prayer, though he had celebrated the sacred mysteries thousands of times since his ordination. They sang the traditional "Beautiful Mother" as the entrance hymn, a couple of verses in English and then, again, in Polish, for those who knew it, the ornate image of the Madonna of Czestochowa behind him. But after the sign of the cross and the opening prayer, Fr. Joe became distracted. He strained to listen to his nephew and niece do the readings, but his mind kept wandering back to Michelle, whose funeral Mass he had celebrated just a few days earlier. Then, he gathered himself to read the Gospel with reverence. When he began to preach, a soft lake breeze moved over the vineyards and through the yard. Within a few minutes, he deviated from his rehearsed homily, amplifying the gospel story about Jesus' healing of the Canaanite woman's daughter in a way he had not intended.

"...And plagued by the demonic, that girl was as good as dead—lost to her mother, lost to herself. But Jesus was moved by that mother's loving entreaty and brought the girl out of the darkness that had tormented her soul and taken a toll on her body." His large hands gestured toward them in empathy and explanation. "He healed her of that fiendish oppression, drawing her into the light, summoning her to a life lived in communion with the saints..."

His extended family sat rapt by the words of their priest, some of the adults wondering what was happening, as if he was saying one thing, but meaning another. Many of the Sadowski children, unable to understand the homily, leaned against their parents, while a few of the teenagers fidgeted on the benches, Uncle Walter's droning somehow harmonious with his godson's words in a kind of inarticulate counterpoint to Fr. Joe's impassioned preaching.

Then the verbal flight was finished. Quoting the psalm response, Fr. Joseph's last words seemed to hover over them momentarily, dissipating with the gentle lake breeze swirling beyond the farmhouse: "...her 'soul rescued like a bird from the fowler's snare,' gathered up in the Holy Trinity, out of time and into eternity."

When a group of his cousins' little children handed him the offertory gifts, he winced at the thought of some rogue priest hurting one of these innocents. Raising the bread and wine in offering to God, as he had done thousands of times before, Fr. Joseph felt a tug in his heart toward the heavens, an inexpressible lifting of his being toward God beyond the beautiful azure sky of summer. During the "Holy, holy, holy" he heard and then saw a honking flock of geese winging their way across the waters, their ordered formation like an arrow piercing the pristine skies. He had a vague, intuitive sense that there was a choir of angels echoing their chant in heaven. While he prayed the Eucharistic Prayer, the intermittent babbling of one of his cousin's babies alternately sharpened or obscured his familial awareness. When it came time to pray the Our Father, Fr. Joe, uncharacteristically, began to sing the words in that ancient chant familiar to the oldest of them. As he consumed the host, he peered into the bloody depth of his chalice for a moment, transfixed by the transubstantiation that he could not perceive. At communion, Fr. Joe was struck with how beautiful they all looked, how graceful and shy, how fragile and radiant. After communion, Fr. Joe sat quietly for a while, a subtle stillness enveloping the familial gathering as the morning's light shone about the vineyards.

When Mass was over, Fr. Joseph changed out of his vestments and purified the vessels in the farmhouse. The men quickly transformed the makeshift church back into a dining area while some of the teenagers set the table and the women made breakfast. Within a few minutes, thermoses of coffee and plates of toast were set out, and then the scrambled eggs and pancakes, the sausages and bacon.

After breakfast, Jenna and Teddy nagged their parents to take them to "Birdland," the preserve on Presque Isle, as they had promised yesterday.

"Okay," Marian said. "Let your father finish his coffee."

On the drive to Presque Isle, Fr. Joseph sat quietly in the front seat with William and Marian. Their two children and a few of their cousins were packed into the SUV. The narrow, mile-long isthmus was on the western side of town, a fifteen-minute ride through Erie on a Sunday morning, past some restaurants and hotels frequented by vacationers. William turned right into the state park. Bicyclers and joggers lined the walkways along the one-way road as they slowly wound their way through the lush isle of trees and foliage, the children's pleasant chatter betraying their excitement.

"There's that Mystery Bay," Teddy said.

"Misery Bay," Marian corrected her son. The children giggled at his mistake. The waterfowl preserve was past the monument site where Admiral Perry and his men had weathered the fierce winter after withstanding the superior British naval contingent in the War of 1812.

Jumping out of the SUV, the children hurried along the narrow path through the brush, William and Marian following behind them, urging them to be quiet. Fr. Joe walked with them for a few yards and then veered off toward the beach.

"I'm going to take a walk along the beach," he said to them over his shoulder, knowing they would have to stay with the children and he could be alone.

The sky was clear and bright as his sandaled feet sank into the smooth, wet sand. He walked past dozens of people lying on the beach, past some children skimming rocks toward the big breakers offshore, past the last lifeguard's chair. When he thought he was alone enough, he started to sing, in a low voice, a few lines he remembered from that haunting Shaker folk song Michelle's friend had sung at her funeral: "The water is wide, I can't cross o'er/ Neither have I wings to fly... A ship there is sails on the sea/ She's loaded deep as deep can be." He was brought out of his melancholic musing when a yellow Frisbee landed at his feet. He picked it up and then flicked it adroitly toward a pretty young woman in a pink bathing suit, her arms and legs glistening with droplets of water. She plucked the hovering Frisbee out of the air. "Thank you," she said and waved as she turned away.

He walked on farther until the last voices of the people were muted by the wind and tide. Alone, now, his sandaled feet planted firmly in the sand, he looked across the wide expanse of the great lake. The air was thin and, squinting his eyes, he tried to discern the faint line of land at the horizon. For a moment, he thought he saw something like a promontory jutting out and above the coastline of Toronto, where the Pope had been last month. He looked up into the blue sky adorned with iridescent clouds shimmering in the sunlight. As he had done hundreds of times before, he peered across Lake Erie and wondered what awaited him on the other side. The slow, rhythmic roll of the lake tide soothed his thoughts like the deep, vibrating pluck of a resonant bass fiddle and helped him await what he sensed coming on the lake breeze. He prayed to God in silence for Michelle's soul, for the souls of his deceased parents, for his godparents and cousins, his aunts and uncles, for all of them. As he gazed at the bright blue sky and darker green waters, the horizon seemed to blur into a kind of ethereal endlessness. The smell of the lake was somehow diffused, now, too. Drawn by the tide's inexorable pull, he lost sense of time and then thought he heard a soft, maternal voice whispering to him on the faint breeze that barely kissed his skin.

Wavering between the here-and-now and the then-and-there, eventually he noticed the white gulls bobbing on the undulating water of the lake: a large one and a small flock of smaller ones, a stone's throw from where he stood. He saw the larger one take flight and the others following him low over the heaving waters. Intently, he watched them winging out across Lake Erie until their croaking died away and they became mere white wisps against the bright blue sky. As they faded beyond his sight, he remembered his dream with the doves and Michelle rising from the frothing waters into the enfolding, blue mantle of the Blessed

Mother. Tears welled up in his eyes. He longed to follow them across the deep.

"Hey, you ready to go?" he heard William's voice calling him back. "The kids didn't see much; just some ducks and a few nestlings with a mother egret."

As they walked quietly back to the SUV, Fr. Joseph could not hear his cousin well, the words sounded garbled in his ears. William noticed Fr. Joe's distracted countenance.

"You look like you saw a ghost, or something," William said. "Are you all right?"

"I saw the gulls flying across the lake," Fr. Joe muttered and slid into the front seat next to Marian. He felt like he had returned from a long voyage at sea and everything seemed unfamiliar.

"You gotta get out more," William teased his cousin, as he got in on the driver's side.

His wife poked him in the ribs with her elbow as he started the car. "He's probably thinking about that girl he buried," Marian whispered to her husband, her words muffled by the cackling of the children playing in the back seat.

And while she was close to the truth of it, they would not have fathomed the serene coast of saints and angels that beckoned to him across the waters of death and awaited them all beyond the great, green lake on the other side of the horizon.

SAINTS AND SOJOURNERS

First Day

He was the last of them to arrive at the Lackawanna shrine; but, then, he was regularly late—as was to be expected, he often quipped, of a "later vocation." Fr. Malcolm had not seen his classmates in quite a while, though they had kept in touch with Christmas cards, emails, texts, and an occasional phone call. Their pastoral duties and personal struggles had consumed the three of them these past several years and, unlike those first few years when they had returned from Rome and taken summer vacations or retreats together, they had drifted apart shortly after the death of Pope John Paul II. And now, it was his recent beatification in Rome that prompted them to get in touch again and plan this pilgrimage across upstate New York in the twelfth year since their ordinations.

As he turned his forest green Jeep Cherokee into the parking lot of Our Lady of Victory Basilica, he glimpsed the indigo eagle's claw that extended to his left forearm below the rolled up sleeve of his plaid flannel shirt, part of the tattoo that began on his bicep, wondering how he was going to explain it to his friends. He parked alongside one of those new Smart Cars, a yellow one with a Canadian license plate, that was half the size of his Jeep. He took a last drag of his cigar then stubbed it out in the ashtray.

When he opened the door to the gift shop in the crypt of the basilica, a little bell jingled. A young man of slight build perusing the bookshelves in drab casual clothing was quick to turn toward the door. They nodded to each other across the little gift shop.

"At least you got the day right," Fr. Louis teased Fr. Malcolm as they shook hands in the middle of the store.

"Only half an hour late, Big Lou," Fr. Malcolm said, using the nickname he had given him after that softball game at the North American College in Rome.

"I arrived last night." Fr. Louis did not mind the nickname, though it was a bit ironic since he was the shortest of them. "I celebrated the early Mass; he has the noon."

As they ascended the marble stairs worn from the shoes of tens of thousands of pilgrims over the decades, they could hear the low murmur of the Our Father emanating from the lunch hour congregation. A couple of steps behind Fr. Malcolm on the stairway, Fr. Louis noticed the dark ponytail dangling over his shirt collar and then the eagle's claw on his forearm.

Stopping on the landing, Fr. Louis asked: "Malcolm, what's that on your arm?"

"Nothin'," he said, self-conscious and a little irritated with the inspection in the basilica. He rolled his shirt sleeves down and buttoned the cuffs. "I'll tell you about it later."

As they slid into the dark mahogany pews, anonymous in their street clothes, they saw Fr. Regis consume the host at the main altar, then the chalice of Christ's blood, beneath the baldacchino with the larger-than-life-sized statue of Our Lady of Victory supported by the columns of rich red marble. The people started moving to the center aisle to receive communion. The two priests noted that there were well over a hundred people in the basilica for this noon Mass on a Monday.

Sitting quietly while the men and women received communion, the priests glanced around the majestic basilica with its painted dome, colorful marble pillars, carved pews, lifelike statues and gold leaf trim on every arch or edge. While they had both been here before, they were still amazed by the basilica's history—how Monsignor Baker had built and paid for this remarkable house of God outside Buffalo, with a national mail-solicitation campaign through the lean years of the depression. Then, they stood up for the closing prayer, Fr. Regis invoking St. Ignatius, bishop of the ancient See of Antioch.

After the final blessing and dismissal, Fr. Regis led the people in the prayer to Our Lady of Victory and a prayer for the beatification of Fr. Baker, Servant of God. Fr. Louis fumbled in the pew rack, finding the laminated card amidst the hymnal and missalettes, a little too late to join in the prayers. As the people walked out of the basilica, Fr. Malcolm moved over for a closer look at the life-sized, marble stations of the cross depicting one of Jesus' falls that stood in relief before the radiant stained glass windows and the colorful mosaic of angels. Fr. Louis, meanwhile, was drawn to the basilica's dome, more than a hundred feet above the sanctuary, its brilliant mosaic depicting the Blessed Virgin Mary's Assumption as she is carried heavenward by the angelic hosts and crowned by the Holy Trinity.

As he came out of the sacristy in his black clerical clothes, Fr. Regis saw Fr. Louis admiring the dome. "Did he get here yet?"

"*Oui*," Fr. Louis said turning toward his friend. 'This place is more beautiful each time I see it."

"Regis," Fr. Malcolm said as he met them at the sanctuary and shook his hand, noticing more gray in his friend's salt and pepper hair. "So when was Fr. Baker declared venerable?"

"Just this January," Fr. Regis explained. "Pope Benedict mentioned his charitable works in the decree. It was a big deal around here. Don't you get news of the universal church in that forest you live in?"

"Last year I accompanied the bishop with our diocesan delegation to Rome for the canonization of Brother Andre Bessette," Fr. Louis said. "*C'etait magnifique.*"

"The little porter at the University of Montreal?" Fr. Malcolm said.

"A million people paid their respects when he died," Fr. Louis said. "He built the largest church dedicated to St. Joseph in the world."

"I just need a few minutes to change and get my things," Fr. Regis said as they walked out of the basilica into the bright fall day. "Whose car do you want to take?"

"My Jeep can hold our suitcases and bags," Fr. Malcolm offered. "But the ride's a little rough."

"We could take my Cadillac," Fr. Regis said. "Smooth ride, roomy, GPS."

"Sounds good," Fr. Louis said.

"Do you guys mind if we take the Cherokee?" Fr. Malcolm asked. "I feel like driving."

"It's okay with me," Fr. Regis said.

"*Moi aussi*," Fr. Louis said as they walked across the parking lot.

"So, what does the bishop think about the ponytail?" Fr. Regis teased his friend.

"I don't think he's seen it yet," Fr. Malcolm said and pointed to the yellow Smart Car parked next to his Jeep. "Does this come with training wheels?"

"It's a rental," Fr. Louis said, enjoying the friendly banter. "I took the whisper train along Lake Ontario from Montreal to Toronto and picked it up for the ride here yesterday."

"Can you guys get the bags?" Fr. Regis asked as they stepped up onto the porch.

Once in the rectory, Fr. Regis went to the office to check his phone messages for any calls from the chancery. His friends went upstairs to get the luggage. Fr. Louis got his bags from the guest room while Fr. Malcolm picked up Fr. Regis' suitcase in front of his door. When they returned to the parking lot, Fr. Malcolm moved his suitcase and some bats, softballs, and a couple of baseball gloves to make room for their luggage in the back of his Jeep. In a few minutes, Fr. Regis joined them, wearing a powder-blue long-sleeved shirt and tan jacket with his black pants. As he got in, he threw a small travel bag over the back seat.

"Everything's an emergency with him," Fr. Regis muttered in frustration as Fr. Malcolm started the car.

"Who?" Fr. Malcolm said.

"Him," Fr. Louis said, making a discreet wave of his hand to indicate to his friend not to pursue the subject of the bishop, which had dominated their conversation over breakfast that morning.

Fr. Malcolm put on the radio, the weather station announcing fifty-five degrees and sunshine for Buffalo and vicinity. Circumventing the city, they drove silently for a while, save for the local news on the radio.

"What's this?" Fr. Louis said as they drove toward the interstate entrance, anxious to redirect their conversation. He touched the webbed hoop and beaded feathers dangling from the rearview mirror of his Jeep.

"It's a dreamcatcher," Fr. Malcolm said. "The plains Indians believed they could sift the good dreams from the bad."

"Since when did you become interested in Indian folklore?" Fr. Regis leaned forward from the back seat.

"Since I found out that I am part Native American." Fr. Malcolm veered onto Interstate 90. "I'm one-sixteenth Seneca. They had settlements all through here. I think it was providential that the bishop assigned me to Tionesta; there's a big Indian festival every August. That's where I bought it."

"With a name like O'Shea?" Fr. Regis voiced his incredulity.

"My great-great-grandfather married a beautiful Indian woman after his first wife and baby died during childbirth," Fr. Malcolm explained as they sped along the highway. "The story goes that he gave three horses, two goats and a rifle for her because she was the chief's daughter."

The other priests chuckled at the story they took to be apocryphal.

"So, you're descended from royalty," Fr. Regis teased him.

"I met an old Indian at the festival a couple of years ago," Fr. Malcolm persisted. "He recognized my family name."

"Did he tell you to grow this thing, too?" Fr. Regis flicked at his ponytail with his finger.

"Look at those mountains," Fr. Louis exclaimed.

The October mountains on either side of Interstate 90 were ablaze in autumn colors: the trees randomly alternating in shades of orange, yellow, red, rust, and some remnant green.

"That is beautiful," Fr. Malcolm said.

"We picked the ideal week for the pilgrimage," Fr. Regis said from the back seat. "The colors are at their peak."

As they drove in silence, enjoying the rich array of fall colors displayed across the rolling hills, Fr. Malcolm thought of Leah, the striking Indian woman he had met at the August festival, her long, raven-black hair, the lightly colored skin, and those dark, shining eyes like

113

smoldering coals in a campfire. He had been instructing her and a couple of others from the chapel church in Tidioute for the past few weeks for the RCIA. But his attraction to her, he knew, was more than paternal.

Driving fast on I-90 in the middle of the day, they had the road to themselves for a while until a New York State Police car pulled up alongside the Jeep in the other lane and the trooper stared at Fr. Malcolm.

"You better slow down some," Fr. Regis said.

"I don't think he likes my ponytail, either," Fr. Malcolm said. He took his foot off the gas pedal to fall back a little and turned off the radio.

The patrol car passed them.

"Do you guys want to stop for lunch someplace?" Fr. Malcolm asked.

"Can you wait until we're closer to Rochester?" Fr. Regis interjected. "There's a good little restaurant not far off the interstate just south of the city; it's less than an hour away."

"I can wait," Fr. Malcolm said.

"Fine," Fr. Louis said.

The prospect of lunch seemed to ease their conversation and they began talking about their work in the Church the past few years: Fr. Louis as retreat director at the diocesan spirituality center in Montreal; Fr. Regis in the canon law office of the Buffalo chancery, working on the cause of venerable Msgr. Baker among a myriad of other tasks; Fr. Malcolm in the middle of the Allegheny National Forest with a parish in Tionesta and a mission in Tidioute. They were catching up for the past few years, exchanging stories about the new generation of seminarians, chancery politics, Pope Benedict and the upcoming translation of the Roman Missal, and then, finally, about fishing for souls along the St. Lawrence Seaway, Lake Erie, and the Allegheny River.

They got to Donato's Restaurant after the lunch-hour crowd had mostly left. Fr. Regis said the blessing. As promised, the food in the small family restaurant was delicious, the service friendly. They enjoyed a bottle of *pinot grigio* with the lake-trout special, some wild rice, and tender brussel sprouts. In the middle of the leisurely afternoon on the first day of their pilgrimage, they had the place to themselves except for an elderly couple and a business group finishing their working lunch. Their conversation ranged from one topic to another as they continued to get reacquainted over their meal. When they were leaving the restaurant, they saw a picture of Archbishop Fulton Sheen hanging on the wall behind the cash register.

"How did you ever find this place?" Fr. Malcolm asked as they returned to his Jeep.

"I have to go to Rochester periodically to help with some projects," Fr. Regis said. "They told me it was one of Archbishop Sheen's favorite places to have a quiet meal with friends."

"Are you working on his cause, too?" Fr. Louis asked as they pulled out of the parking lot.

"I'm not supposed to talk about it," Fr. Regis said.

"I heard that the miracle was in Pittsburgh," Fr. Malcolm said.

"One of them," Fr. Regis said. "Who knows? He could be beatified in a few years."

The mention of the early Catholic televangelist's pending cause for sainthood drew Fr. Louis into a silent introspection as he looked out onto the seemingly endless mountain ranges, dappled with extravagant color, on either side of the interstate. He wondered if that powerful preacher with the piercing blue eyes had known the aridity that plagued his own prayer life—if the archbishop ever had a pro-longed period of acedia, as he had been strug-gling with for more than a year now.

Fr. Regis reached behind the seat and grabbed the small overnight bag he had thrown on the luggage. "Louis, play this," he said and handed him a compact disc between the front seats. "It'll be great for the ride to Syracuse. It's Copland's *Appalachian Spring Suite*; it's one of my favorite pieces of classical music."

"Sure." Fr. Louis placed the disc in the dash-board CD player.

The sky shone bright and blue with the sun-light spangling across the highway as they drove east above the Finger Lakes named for the ancient tribes that first inhabited these lands, like Seneca and Cayuga. So many Indian names for towns or waters survived in this part of upstate New York, that it gave the region a kind of ancient, mythical quality. The valley drive between the resplendent mountain ranges, suitably accompanied by the New York Philharmonic, relaxed the three friends, enabling them to decompress from their priestly duties and anxieties, enchanting them into a kind of elemental mood of freedom that they had seldom experienced in recent years. They had the good sense not to talk, letting the masterful orchestral recording and the natural palate of vibrant fall colors wash over their senses on this beautiful day for a drive across the picturesque American landscape.

With the last still, slow note of the suite lingering in the car, Fr. Louis exhaled deeply, as if loosening the knotted emotions in his mind and body that had constrained his prayer life these past many months.

"I think I recognized that melody in the middle," Fr. Malcolm said.

"It's an old Shaker tune," Fr. Regis explained. "We sing a version of it at Mass: 'The Lord of the Dance.'"

"I knew it was familiar," Fr. Malcolm said as he passed a large truck on the highway.

"Do you guys remember the trip we took to Turin when they put the Shroud on display?" Fr. Louis asked, not waiting for their answer. "I saw a video at the center a few weeks ago that said they did some tests on it here in upstate New York at some kind of research facility. I think it was MacBeth Studios."

"Kodak's in Rochester," Fr. Regis said. "Was that on PBS?"

"I don't know about in the States," Fr. Louis said and gestured with his hands for emphasis. "It was fascinating. They said the image on the Shroud was like a photographic negative, as if the light emanated out of the body onto the cloth, leaving a negative impression of the man. Somehow, with computer aided analysis, they reconfigured the body with all of the wounds and produced a three-dimensional image of Christ crucified."

"If it is Jesus," Fr. Regis said. "I thought there was some problem with the carbon dating."

"They had some scientific explanation for the discrepancy," Fr. Louis said. "Something about the handling of the cloth over the years."

The Jeep went over a bump in the road or a dead animal and they were all jostled in their seats.

"Syracuse is less than an hour away," Fr. Malcolm said. "We're probably going to hit the rush hour."

"Do you guys want to stop at a casino for supper and a little gambling?" Fr. Regis asked. "There's a resort a few miles south of Syracuse off of I-81 on the Onondaga Reservation," Fr. Regis read from his AAA brochure in the back seat. "Malcolm, you would be supporting your people."

"Onondaga?" Fr. Malcolm perked up. "That's the place the Five Nations formed the

Iroquois Confederacy that ruled this region for centuries before the French and English."

"You have been brushing up on your Native American history," Fr. Louis said.

"I've been reading a book that retells their oral tradition," Fr. Malcolm said. "The Iroquois Book of Life."

"Well, if we want to go," Fr. Regis continued, "we have to take this bypass coming up to get on 81 South."

"I'm not hungry, yet," Fr. Louis said.

"Yeah, me neither," Fr. Malcolm said.

"There's another one about forty miles or so from here, just off 90," Fr. Regis explained from the brochure. "It's a big resort run by the Oneida Nation: Turning Leaf Casino."

"Let's keep driving," Fr. Malcolm said. "That sounds about right."

"Can we still get to Cooperstown tonight?" Fr. Louis asked.

"It's only a couple hours away," Fr. Regis assured him. "We have reservations for a couple nights at a motel right on the lake. Don't worry."

They drove east awhile on the interstate until the heavy Syracuse rush-hour traffic dissipated behind them.

"Isn't Syracuse the place where Sister Mary Ann Cope's order was from?" Fr. Louis wondered aloud.

"Who?" Fr. Malcolm asked.

"She's the nun who went to Molokai to help Fr. Damien with the lepers," Fr. Regis said. "They were a nursing order from Syracuse."

"*Oui*," Fr. Louis said. "Franciscans."

"She's already blessed," Fr. Regis explained. "I remember reading about her cause—she could be canonized in a few years."

"What about you, Big Lou?" Fr. Malcolm teased his friend. "I'll write a testimonial on your behalf."

"They'll reject it because you're tattooed," Fr. Louis teased him back. "You defaced your body like a pagan."

"What tattoo?" Fr. Regis asked.

"Thanks." Fr. Malcolm glanced at Fr. Louis. "I got one at the Indian festival in August. The old man called me Little Eagle. I had a little too much to drink one night and got an eagle tattooed on my left arm."

"Let me see," Fr. Regis said.

"Wait till we get out," Fr. Malcolm said.

"You painted heathen," Fr. Regis teased him.

"Thanks, Lou," Fr. Malcolm said. "Now, I'll have to listen to this all across New York."

"Do you guys want to pray vespers?" Fr. Louis asked, noticing the waning light of the approaching dusk sky.

"Might as well," Fr. Malcolm said, anxious to change the subject.

Fr. Regis reached in the back of the Jeep to get their breviaries from the overnight bags.

He handed his to his friend in the front seat. Fr. Louis led their antiphonal prayer for the feast of St. Ignatius, father and martyr of the early Church, with Fr. Regis doing the readings and petitions and Fr. Malcolm joining in when he knew the psalm by heart. During their five years in Rome, they had prayed the office together hundreds of times.

It was dusk by the time they reached the exit for the Oneida resort, the same exit as for the town of Rome.

"Now, there's a sign that God has a sense of humor," Fr. Malcolm said as he turned onto the exit ramp. "Three Catholic priests on the way to Rome stopped at an Indian casino..."

"Sounds like the opening line of some joke," Fr. Regis said.

"Why are the casinos on the reservations?" Fr. Louis asked.

"They're exempt from taxes," Fr. Regis said. "Over the years, they've made a killing—kind of a reversal of roles by a conquered people."

Fr. Malcolm followed the signs to the Turning Leaf Resort. In a few minutes, they saw the lighted complex of hotels, restaurants, shops, and casinos. Fr. Malcolm parked the Jeep, and they walked to the nearest resort building.

"Let's try our luck before we eat," Fr. Regis said.

"Whoever wins buys dinner and drinks," Fr. Malcolm said as they passed two security guards at the casino entrance. Inside, they stopped to survey the milling crowd swarming around the tables and spinning wheels, lining up at the orderly rows of slot machines. Against the steady murmur of the hundreds of voices, an occasional bell or whistle or celebrative exclamation rose above the droning din.

"I'll just wait here for you guys," Fr. Louis said, overwhelmed by his first experience of a gaming floor. "The carpet is so ugly."

"Louis, do you have some quarters or ones?" Fr. Regis asked. "You can play the slot machines and not lose more than ten or twenty dollars."

"I'm going to play some black jack," Fr. Malcolm said and went into the crowd toward the back where the tables were.

"I'm going to play some poker. Louis, try one of those," Fr. Regis said, pointing to a nearby row of empty slot machines. "I'll meet you back here in about half an hour or so, unless I'm winning."

Fr. Louis watched Fr. Regis walking between a couple of rows of slot machines toward the poker room in the corner of the expansive casino floor. He noticed that there seemed to be no windows to look out of while he waited for his friends. He had never cared much for gambling, even modest games like church bingo. It wasn't a moral issue for him so much as a lack of familiarity, and so he never understood the attraction. His only real experience with gambling was in the confessional when he would scold the men or women who wasted their family's precious money on sports betting or lottery tickets. He knew he was out of his element when he had to fill in and give a weekend retreat to that Gamblers Anonymous group at the center last year because their regular chaplain had an allergic reaction to the clam sauce on the linguini at Raffaele's. Those poor people, he thought, recalling their blank faces as he spoke about the purgative, illuminative, and unitive ways in the weekend conferences.

"Here goes nothing," Fr. Louis muttered the phrase he learned from his American friends at the NAC as he slid his dollar into the nearby slot machine with the western motif.

"Would you like a drink while you're playing?" a petite waitress asked him, seemingly coming out of nowhere.

"A glass of *chenin blanc, merci*," Fr. Louis said nervously. He watched the drum spin and stop with no match: a turtle, a deer and a rabbit. He tried a few more times but to no avail.

"Is this your first time at the casino?" the young waitress asked returning with his white wine.

"I'm here with some friends who like to gamble," he said. "I'm just trying my luck while I'm waiting for them."

Hearing the bells and whistles resounding on a slot machine in the center of the floor, Fr. Louis knew that someone was winning.

"You can increase the jackpot if you push the button that says 'MAX'," the waitress explained. "But the odds of winning become more difficult."

"This one?" Fr. Louis pushed the big, red button with his finger. He slid another dollar into the slot machine.

The pretty waitress stood beside him.

When he lost again, Fr. Louis took a sip of the refreshing wine and, then, realizing the etiquette, placed a couple of dollars on her tray.

"Thank you." The waitress smiled and turned away. "Good luck."

He tried a few more dollars but with the same result.

"*C'est la vie*," he took a sip of wine and placed his last dollar bill in the slot machine. He watched the three drums spin and then stop, one after the other: buffalo, buffalo, buffalo. The lights on the machine began flashing and then it emitted a high-pitched whistling sound. He knew that he had won.

"You won!" The waitress returned. "Now take that slip of paper to the cashier in the back there."

A few people nearby took notice of his winning and nodded their approval, quickly returning their attention to their own machines.

"*Mon Dieu!*" Fr. Louis exclaimed and gulped his wine, placing the empty glass on her tray. "Where do I go?"

"C'mon, I'll show you." She seemed as delighted as he was.

Fr. Louis read aloud the figure on the slip of paper as she led him through the crowd. "It says I've won eight hundred and fifty dollars."

"See, I told you, you have to take a risk to win big," the waitress reminded him. "There's the cashier. We're not allowed to go up with the players."

"*Sil vous plait,*" Fr. Louis said. "I'll be right back."

Fr. Louis collected his winnings at the window and returned to the helpful waitress. He placed one of the fifty-dollar bills on her tray. "*Merci.*"

"Thank you!" She smiled at him and disappeared into the crowd.

Fr. Louis returned to the front of the room to wait for his friends, wondering if they had fared as well. Fr. Malcolm was the first to return.

"How did it go?" Fr. Malcolm asked.

"Not bad for the first time," Fr. Louis said. "How did you do?"

"I only lost forty dollars," he said. "I got blackjack a couple of times."

The two priests watched as Fr. Regis walked toward them slowly, his hands in his pockets.

"How much did you lose, Rege?" Fr. Malcolm asked.

"Only fifty bucks," he said.

"I lost forty," Fr. Malcolm said.

"Did you try the slots?" Fr. Regis asked Fr. Louis.

"I did well enough," he said.

"How well?" Fr. Malcolm pushed.

"Eight-fifty," Fr. Louis said.

"You won eight-fifty playing the quarter slots?" Fr. Regis said. "That's not bad for the first time."

"No," Fr. Louis smiled broadly. "Eight hundred fifty on the dollar ones."

"Big Lou," Fr. Malcolm slapped him on his back.

"Way to go, Louis," Fr. Regis said.

"So, where do you guys want to eat?" Fr. Louis asked. "I'm buying supper!"

"Yes, you are," Fr. Malcolm said, slapping him on the back, again.

"The best restaurant is upstairs, c'mon," Fr. Regis said, laughing as they made their way to the elevator. "Eight hundred fifty!"

"Not bad for some pious priest from Canada," Fr. Malcolm said as they got out of the elevator. "I could go for a good steak."

And it was at that casino supper, near the end of the first day of their pilgrimage, that time seemed to slow and space contract as they relived dozens of similar meals they had shared more than a decade ago, on the other side of the Atlantic, when they were seminarians studying at the North American College and traveled by rail to Assisi or Venice, Lourdes or Paris, Berlin or Munich, Madrid or Fatima, and then by ferry to Dublin or London, on weekend excursions across that European continent that had held their imaginations' interest since they were boys old enough to read about kings and knights, castles and monasteries, wars and revolutions, schisms and reformations, about an armored pope on horseback turning back the pagan horde at the gates of Rome, about the western civilization that had formed their family lineages and through which their priestly vocations had taken shape. And while the second bottle of *cabernet sauvignon* assisted their traverse to that other time and place, their rich laughter was more delicious than the

filet mignon and warm buttered bread they enjoyed as they basked in the fraternity that had
brought them together to serve Christ in the
Church as priests of the God who had whispered their names into His bold service.
Through the recollection of ancient gothic
cathedrals, Fr. Regis had forgotten about negotiating chancery politics and personalities.
With the remembered voices of timeless
monastic choirs, the aridity of Fr. Louis'
prayer was washed away for a while. Recalling
the aching beauty of murals, marble statues and
mosaics, Fr. Malcolm's guilty attraction to a
comely, young woman seemed nothing more
than an innocent, passing glance. Grace was
like that: deftly transforming realities beyond
their wildest imaginings. And, besides all that,
the effortless ease of the wager, the found
money that funded their evening's fellowship,
seemed right and necessary, a gracious and in-

135

explicable gift, free and, therefore, almost providential.

"We get 28 South at Mohawk up here a couple of miles," Fr. Regis said, studying the map with the help of the overhead light shining above the front seat of the Jeep.

"Is he sleeping?" Fr. Louis asked from behind the steering wheel.

"He went out twenty miles ago," Fr. Regis said. "We'll be in Cooperstown in half an hour. This is it—take this exit."

The state road was a slower drive as the two lanes wound through some small towns and unlit farm fields. Fr. Louis recounted the diocesan pilgrimage he led last year to the Canadian shrine of the North American Martyrs in Midland, Ontario, but Fr. Regis was beginning to doze. Within the hour, he was turning the Jeep off of Main Street and into the parking lot of the Lakeside Motel. He handed the sleepy Fr. Regis a few fifty dollar bills to cover their stay.

"God will provide," Fr. Louis joked and woke Fr. Malcolm in the back seat. "You'll have to go with Regis to identify the vehicle." He collected their bags and luggage while they took care of the reservations and room keys at the office.

"We're in this one: 9-A." Fr. Regis handed Fr. Malcolm his key. "Louis, you have the single next door, 9-B. You paid for them."

"Goodnight," they said and carried their bags into their rooms for the welcomed night's rest.

Second Day

The morning on Lake Otsego was cool and damp as the three priests woke slowly from their sound sleep in Cooperstown on this, the second day of their pilgrimage.

"How did you sleep, Louis?" Fr. Regis asked as he opened their door.

"*Per le morte*," Fr. Louis said.

"I was out as soon as my head hit the pillow," Fr. Regis said, continuing to button his blue golf shirt. "He's in the shower."

"Do you want to get some breakfast?" Fr. Louis asked. "I'm still buying."

"We have a lot of time," Fr. Regis said. "The Hall's opened until five o'clock."

Fr. Malcolm came out of the bathroom with a white towel wrapped around his waist.

"Too much firewater, chief?" Fr. Regis said.

Fr. Malcolm ignored the teasing.

"Hey, there it is." Fr. Regis took a couple of steps toward him to get a better look at the indigo eagle tattoo on Fr. Malcolm's arm.

"Did it hurt?" Fr. Louis asked.

"I wasn't feeling much pain that night," Fr. Malcolm said.

"You got it at some Indian festival?" Fr. Regis held his wrist and straightened his forearm to get a better look at the iconic image.

"The old man told me it was like a tribal crest or something..." Fr. Malcolm moved his arm out of Fr. Regis' grasp "...on my great-great-grandmother's side."

"It's pretty cool," Fr. Regis said.

"Tell my mother," Fr. Malcolm said. "She dislikes the ponytail, too. I got to get ready."

"We'll be outside," Fr. Regis said. "We're going out for breakfast."

"Do you want to pray morning prayer?" Fr. Regis asked Fr. Louis once they were outside. "It's the feast of St. Luke."

"*Oui*," Fr. Louis said. "And we can have Mass in my room later this afternoon after the Hall tour. I brought a Mass kit with a host and wine."

After a few more minutes, Fr. Malcolm, in blue jeans, a flannel shirt and Dockers, joined them on the walkway that fronted their rooms.

"Do you want to pray morning prayer before we go for breakfast?" Fr. Regis asked him.

"I need some coffee before I can face God," Fr. Malcolm said, giving his friends a little laugh as they walked to the diner on Main Street.

They enjoyed the hearty Homerun Breakfast of eggs, toast, pancakes, bacon, potatoes, coffee, and juice, though Fr. Louis would have preferred the light crepes with fresh fruit preserves and espresso that were commonplace on menus in Montreal. The coffee was strong and the waitress kept their cups full as they discussed the day's itinerary across the table in the Homeplate Diner.

"So, why are you so gung ho about baseball?" Fr. Malcolm asked Fr. Louis. "As I remember, you had never picked up a bat until that game at the NAC."

"Momen Clemente," Fr. Louis said.

"You mean Roberto?" Fr. Regis asked.

"Before he played for the Pittsburgh team, he was on the Montreal Royals," Fr. Louis explained. "My father met him in 1954 while he was a graduate student in romance languages and literature at the university. Momen was his nickname among the Latin players."

"I thought the Expos used to be Montreal's team," Fr. Malcolm said.

"This was before that," Fr. Louis said. "They were a farm team of the Brooklyn Badgers —"

"— Dodgers," Fr. Regis corrected him.

"Whatever," Fr. Louis said, anxious to continue his story.

"They put Clemente in the Hall of Fame right after he died in that airplane crash taking supplies to earthquake victims in Nicaragua," Fr. Malcolm said.

"They waived the five-year waiting period for him like the Church did for St. Francis," Fr. Regis added.

"Well," Fr. Louis said and took an impatient sip of his coffee. "When he got to Montreal he couldn't speak any English, let alone French. So the Royals asked the university for a tutor, and my father, who was fluent in English, French, and Italian, as well as Spanish, helped him with his language that season."

"Really?" Fr. Malcolm said.

"It was a short time—just a few months," Fr. Louis said. "But Clemente became my father's favorite professional athlete. After that summer, he followed his career in Pittsburgh. When I was growing up, the professor made us watch reruns of the World Series the couple of times the Pirates were in it so he could tell stories about Momen Clemente to me and my brothers and sisters."

"That's some story," Fr. Regis said.

"*Mon père* told me that Clemente converted to Catholicism when he got married—he may have been Baptist or something," Fr. Louis continued. "He told us that he took him to see St. Joseph Oratory near the university once; and, as they prayed at the crypt of Brother Andre, Clemente was deeply moved with the account of his life's work helping students and the poor of Montreal."

"Well, what do you think?" Fr. Malcolm got up from their table.

"Yeah," Fr. Regis said. "Time to go."

"I want to get my father something that will be a worthy remembrance," Fr. Louis said, pushing his chair away from the table.

"Like a jersey or a hat?" Fr. Regis offered as he stood up.

"I don't know." Fr. Louis left the money for their breakfast and tip on the table. "But I'll know it when I see it. Dr. Dupuis is going to be eighty-four at the end of the month."

When they got back to the motel, they went into Fr. Louis' room to pray the liturgy of the hours on the feast day of St. Luke the Evangelist. Afterwards, they freshened up and walked the couple of blocks to the National Baseball Hall of Fame and Museum.

"Providential," Fr. Regis said and playfully poked Fr. Malcolm's tattooed arm with the admissions ticket. It displayed a picture of Bob Feller in his Cleveland Indians uniform in mid-delivery with that legendary leg kick as high as his head.

"Anglo-American imperialist," Fr. Malcolm teased him back.

"My last name's Peterson," Fr. Regis protested. "I'm German-Irish."

"Even worse," Fr. Malcolm teased.

"Play nice, you two," Fr. Louis said. "Where's the gift shop?"

"We'll have time when we leave," Fr. Regis said. "Let's go upstairs—there's a short movie, the hall plaques, some historical rooms..."

After the film in the multimedia theater, the three priests meandered through exhibits about the nineteenth-century origins of baseball, the Negro leagues, women in the game, a recently unveiled tribute to scouts, and a timeline of the "national pastime" over the last hundred years, or so. Fr. Louis took special notice of any accounts of the Pittsburgh Pirates, anxious to hear about the great Roberto.

"The third floor has the ballparks and the World Series," Fr. Regis said as they ascended the wide staircase with the few other fans there that autumn morning.

"Sacred ground?" Fr. Louis read incredulously as they walked into the gallery of ballparks.

"With us," Fr. Regis said, "the fields are almost like churches—Wrigley Field, Yankee Stadium, Fenway Park...you're Canadian, you don't get it."

"I get it," Fr. Louis teased. "You cretins think going to a baseball game fulfills your Sunday obligation."

"Almost," Fr. Malcolm interjected.

They continued through the World Series exhibit, surveying artifacts, memorabilia and video highlights of the October classic.

"I think the Series starts this week," Fr. Malcolm said.

"The first game is Wednesday night when we get back," Fr. Regis said as they left the gallery.

"Who's playing?" Fr. Louis asked.

"Fellows, come here." Fr. Regis motioned to his friends to come into the next room. "Louis, you have to see this."

They watched an old film clip of entertainers Bud Abbot and Lou Costello doing their famous baseball routine known as "Who's on First?" with its intricate word play, flawless timing, comedic confusion, and those cherubic facial expressions of the little, rotund Costello.

"That's hilarious," Fr. Malcolm said.

"It's over fifty years old, and it's still funny," Fr. Regis said and glanced at Fr. Louis.

"I get it," Fr. Louis said. "The bases: first, second, third..."

"The gift shop is on the first floor," Fr. Regis said. "But first we have to see the hall of fame plaques with all of the inductees. Clemente will be in there."

They hurried through the art display featuring paintings and sculpture representing the game and its heroes.

Once in the large Hall of Fame Gallery, they were faced with the challenge of finding Roberto Clemente's bronze plaque hanging on the oak-lined walls amidst the hundreds of other great players and managers, umpires and owners.

"He was inducted in 1973," Fr. Malcolm said, "a few months after he died in that plane crash."

"New Year's Day, 1973," Fr. Louis said. "I was just a little boy but I remember seeing *mon père* crying when he heard the news."

"They're ordered by the year of induction," Fr. Regis said. "He'll be down the other end."

Fr. Louis started looking on one wall and his friends on the other.

"Big Lou," Fr. Malcolm called across the hall in a hushed voice. "Over here."

Fr. Louis read the inscription on the handsome bronze bas relief of his father's favorite baseball player. Seeing the man's image in this Hall of Fame confirmed and enlivened all of the stories his father had told him over the years about the great Momen Clemente and the Pittsburgh Pirates, champions of baseball in 1960, 1971—and again in 1979, after Clemente had died.

"They beat the vaunted New York Yankees in 1960," Fr. Regis said. "Mantle, Maris, Ford, Berra..."

"I never heard him called 'Roberto Clemente Walker,'" Fr. Malcolm said.

"It was his mother's maiden name," Fr. Louis explained. "That's the way Hispanics order their family names."

"There's a library and bookstore in the next wing," Fr. Regis said. "You could buy your father a biography."

"He's read them all," Fr. Louis said. "He especially liked the most recent one published last year."

"There's a display of baseball movies and props in that other section," Fr. Malcolm said.

"You guys go," Fr. Louis said. "Meet me in the gift shop. I want to find a keepsake for his shelf."

So Fr. Regis and Fr. Malcolm went off to see the documents, books, and films that have become part of the lore of baseball, while Fr. Louis went downstairs.

In the gift shop, Fr. Louis meandered through the aisles and displays until he spotted some figurines of the famous players. He found one of Clemente doffing his Pirates cap as he stood on a base labeled 3,000, the final hit of his illustrious career before his untimely death. He took a few steps with the resin statue in hand and then stopped at a display of baseballs encased in clear plastic and mounted on wooden stands with the busts of the hall's heroes painted on them about the size of a half-dollar. *C'est parfait*, he thought as he sorted through dozens of balls until he found the one with the handsome face of Roberto Clemente painted on the white cover. He put the figurine back on the shelf. He read the display card about the New England artist who hand-painted the faces of many of the game's greatest players on baseballs as a kind of tribute. *He'll love it*, Fr. Louis thought as he approached the cash register.

"Louis, they have packages of all his baseball cards," Fr. Regis said as they met at the counter.

"Thanks, but I already bought him a gift." Fr. Louis took the baseball out of the bag for them to see.

"Cool," Fr. Malcolm said. "It's like a totem."

"Or an icon," Fr. Regis said.

"Mon père will love it," Fr. Louis said. *"C'est parfait!"*

The three priests left the Hall of Fame and walked along Main Street. No one was hungry yet after their big breakfast, so they turned on First Street toward their motel on Lake Otsego.

"Do you want to celebrate Mass this afternoon?" Fr. Louis asked his friends. "I have all the things we need."

"Sure," Fr. Regis said.

"Yeah," Fr. Malcolm said. "We can skip lunch and get an early supper at that steak house we passed."

"Bambino's?" Fr. Regis said. "I've eaten there before. They cook a great steak. We can have a couple beers, too."

"Sounds good," Fr. Malcolm said.

"We'll have a good meal, a good night's rest," Fr. Louis said. "So we can get an early start to the shrine tomorrow."

Back at the motel, Fr. Regis and Fr. Malcolm refreshed themselves. Next door, Fr. Louis prepared for Mass. He took out his Roman Missal and set the ribbons to the Feast of St. Luke the Evangelist. He cleared the low dresser top of odds and ends and then opened the small chaplain's case with the sacred vessels: chalice, paten, crucifix and stand, stoles, corporal and purificator, small bottles of water and wine, a large host, a shallow lavabo bowl, and two candles with holders for the makeshift altar. Assembling these "tools of the trade" in his lake-side motel room, he felt again that dark emptiness that had pervaded his prayer for the past year or so, the dutiful gathering of himself in priestly service without the abiding consolation that he had experienced earlier in his priesthood. Looking in the mirror at his somber face beneath his closely cropped light brown hair, Fr. Louis paused to ask God to help him during this pilgrimage, to refresh his prayer life, to be with him in the celebration of this motel Mass. He was taken out of his desperate prayer by the knock at the door.

"Big Lou," Fr. Malcolm said as they entered his room.

"I'll be ready in a few minutes," Fr. Louis said and set the candles and crucifix, the corporal and vessels in place atop the styleless blond dresser. He angled the Roman Missal on the edge of the purificator. "Do you have any matches?"

Fr. Malcolm lit the candles.

Fr. Louis handed the small stoles to his friends; they were about the size of a man's belt. "I didn't have red ones," he said. The stoles were white on one side and purple on the other to serve a chaplain's need.

They kissed the white side of the stoles at the embroidered cross before laying them around their necks, Fr. Louis in the middle flanked by his friends. The dresser's large mirror reflected their unlikely altar with its unique appointments. They all took note of the quaint arrangement of the holy sacrifice they were about to celebrate.

Fr. Louis recited the introductory and penitential rites in the usual way and tried to enter into the solemnity of the Mass. Something about the mirrored crucifix on the cheap dresser seen from behind distracted them, hindering them all from entering more deeply into the liturgy even as they prayed the Gloria. The readings and psalm response read by Fr. Regis from the missal barely seemed to strengthen their engagement in the profundities they were praying. Fr. Louis' reading of the gospel gave them pause but the spontaneous petitions they offered were prosaic and uninspired. Yet, when Fr. Malcolm handed him the small chalice and paten in silence, the mirrored action of his consecrated hands moved Fr. Louis to drop his voice in reverence for the sacred mysteries taking shape in front of their eyes. The simple action of lifting the paten and chalice, reflected in the mirror, transfixed them in some way as Fr. Louis whispered the words of offering. Even the ablution had a distinct quality, the poured water washing over Fr. Louis' hands and trickling into the small, glass bowl that Fr. Malcolm held. The familiar rhythm of the preface dialogue heightened their participation. They whispered the words of the "Holy, holy, holy" with awareness and piety.

And, as soon as Fr. Louis began the Eucharistic Prayer, the three priests seemed to come together as one, an unspoken empathy causing them to nearly breathe in unison as Fr. Louis prayed aloud on their behalf. The solemn offering of the simple gifts of bread and wine was intensified by their mirrored reflection, as if the consecratory words and actions echoed into a timeless and fathomless depth. "This is my body..." Fr. Louis spoke the sacred words slowly while the others lipped them as if for the first time. "This is the cup of my blood..." Flawlessly, the other priests prayed aloud their parts of the canon, Fr. Malcolm pausing at the name of the local bishop, which Fr. Regis whispered to him. Finishing the long Eucharistic Prayer, their "Amen" reverberated in the small motel room. The Lord's Prayer, the Lamb of God and the Sign of Peace proceeded effortlessly, as if someone or something else empowered the practiced words and made the familiar gestures on their behalf. They no longer noticed the reflected image of their celebration. Consuming the body and blood of Christ, they were blind to their colorless motel surroundings, lost in the communion that held the central meaning of their priestly lives.

Fr. Louis purified the little vessels in a perfunctory way, setting their dresser-top altar as it was when they began the Mass. After the closing prayer and final blessing, the three priests bowed and unconsciously sighed a breath like an harmonic hymn of subtle praise.

His friends helped Fr. Louis reassemble the chaplain's kit neatly in its case and replace the clock radio, tissues and coffee maker on the dresser.

Fr. Regis picked up a book on the nightstand, unable to make out the title. "What are you reading, Louis?"

"*The Three Conversions in the Spiritual Life*, by Garrigou-Lagrange," Fr. Louis said. "In the original French. It's a classic of mystical theology. I think he taught John Paul at the Angelicum."

"One of the things I miss most about Rome," Fr. Malcolm said and stretched his long arms in a broad yawn "...was that little afternoon rest after *pranzo*."

"So civilized," Fr. Regis said.

"Well, we are on pilgrimage," Fr. Louis said. "We ate a late breakfast."

"All right," Fr. Regis said. "It's almost three o'clock. Let's crash for a while and go out to eat at five-thirty or so."

"Great!" Fr. Malcolm said.

Fr. Regis and Fr. Malcolm returned to their room. Fr. Louis closed the blinds on the lone window in his room; and, shortly after his head eased onto the pillow, he was dreaming about a sidewalk café in Paris they had frequented years ago on their excursion to France.

Refreshed from their afternoon's rest, the three priests in fall jackets walked up First Street to Main where they went a block or so past the Hall of Fame to Bambino's Restaurant, named after baseball's legendary Babe Ruth. Having skipped lunch after their late and ample breakfast, they were hungry and looking forward to a good meal in the midst of their pilgrimage, like they always tried to do when they traveled Europe by rail during their years at the NAC.

The restaurant was not crowded, and they were seated readily. Fr. Malcolm and Fr. Regis ordered bottles of a local beer while Fr. Louis preferred a glass of *chardonnay*. When the middle-aged waitress returned with their drinks, Fr. Regis was the first to order.

"I'll have 'The Babe,' medium rare." Fr. Regis ordered the twelve-ounce New York strip steak featured on the menu. "Baked potato, sour cream, and a house salad with Italian dressing."

"Make mine the same and put them on his check," Fr. Malcolm said, pointing to Fr. Louis.

Fr. Louis smiled and nodded to their waitress. "I'll have the veal Romano with a side of penne pasta in marinara sauce with the garden salad and balsamic vinaigrette on the side."

The waitress collected their menus.

"How's the fried zucchini?" Fr. Regis asked.

"It's our specialty," the waitress said, smiling back at Fr. Regis' handsome face. "Paper thin and lightly breaded."

"Enough for the three of us?" Fr. Malcolm asked.

"Plenty," she said. "I'll put the appetizer in first before your dinners."

Toasting their pilgrimage reunion, the three priests fell into that easy conversation that had characterized their years together in Rome. At supper, on this second evening of their trip, they began to let their guard down with each other, revealing glimpses of the struggles and frustrations they had encountered those dozen years since their bishops had laid hands on their heads. They deftly changed the subject when their waitress returned with their zucchini and dinner rolls. Fr. Louis ordered another round of drinks. While they squeezed lemon or sprinkled cheese on the zucchini, or dipped it in marinara sauce, they picked up the complaints they had begun with their first drinks: Fr. Regis' ongoing tension with his bishop, who was tolerant of the older generation of priests with their liturgical irregularities and criticism of the Vatican; Fr. Louis' strained attempt to balance the needs of his own prayer life with the round of retreats, spiritual direction at the seminary, diocesan pilgrimages, and the seemingly endless line of priests seeking solace from their exhausting duties; and Fr. Malcolm's elliptical reference to the challenge of celibacy as a way of vaguely insinuating his own attraction to that beautiful Indian woman, though he could not yet say it aloud. When their waitress brought their meals, they ordered another round of drinks, since they weren't driving, and the three priests continued their discussion even as the restaurant began to fill with patrons. More than once, Fr. Regis had to remind his friends to lower their voices. They enjoyed the juicy steaks covered with mushrooms and onions and the thin, lightly battered veal. When they finished their delicious suppers, they turned down the waitress' offer of dessert and coffee and, instead, ordered a last round of beers and wine. Relishing their renewed camaraderie, they made a final toast to the North American College that had brought them together in Rome for five of the best years of their lives. Fr. Louis left the money for the check on the table with a generous tip for their attentive waitress. Outside in the fresh autumn air, the night's chill roused them from their torpor of food and drink, and they paused a moment, looking for a little adventure.

"Doubleday Field is just up there a ways." Fr. Regis pointed to the wide walkway that led to the ballpark used for the annual Hall of Fame Game. "It's a nice night."

"I could go for a little stroll," Fr. Louis said.

"Those beers got to me," Fr. Malcolm said and turned down Main Street in the opposite direction toward their motel. "I gotta piss like a race horse."

"C'mon, Lou," Fr. Regis said. "He'll catch up."

The two priests meandered along the generous pavement, stopping at the statue of a little boy, bat in hand, poised to hit. Other people were also admiring the charming statue.

"So, you guys never played baseball when you were kids?" Fr. Regis asked his friend.

"Hockey," Fr. Louis said. "Soccer, too. The Montreal Canadiens were like the New York Yankees when we were growing up."

They stood chatting awhile near the statue, watching the families ambling about in the cool October night, the young children giddy with excitement. As they continued their walk, they could see the entrance to Doubleday Field.

"Why Doubleday Field?" Fr. Louis asked.

"Abner Doubleday was the guy who supposedly invented the game of baseball," Fr. Regis said. "They had town teams all through upstate New York. It was in the film at the Hall."

"If *mon père* had not known the great Clemente," Fr. Louis said, "I doubt if we would have ever talked about baseball at home."

"Well, whaddaya say?" Fr. Malcolm said, standing in front of them with a couple of gloves, a softball and a bat in his hands, a lit cigar dangling from the corner of his mouth.

"What?" Fr. Regis said.

"Let's play some ball," Fr. Malcolm said.

"You had one too many beers there, fella," Fr. Regis said, feeling the effects of the beer now, too.

"The gate's open, c'mon," Fr. Malcolm insisted.

"Are we allowed on the field?" Fr. Louis asked.

"There's no signs saying we're not," Fr. Malcolm said, his broad back obscuring the sign prohibiting trespassers. "I parked by the stands and the gate's unlocked. There's even a couple of lights on."

"What do you think, Big Lou?" Fr. Regis said. "It'll be like that time at the *campo sportivo* that first spring—remember you got the big hit that brought Malcolm home to beat the guys from the Angelicum."

"It was a triple to right center like the great Clemente used to hit," Fr. Louis recalled.

"Well," Fr. Regis said. "More like a single and a two-base error but we won the game—that's all that matters."

"Just for a little while, Big Lou," Fr. Malcolm said. "What can happen?"

And if they had not been drinking, they would have remembered the last time that Fr. Malcolm had dared them to push the limit, during their trip to Medjugorje more than a dozen years ago, when they were detained for a couple of hours due to their laughter and high spirits at the border of Croatia and Bosnia-Herzegovinia, when they all had to get out of the bus while their bags were searched and before they were eventually allowed to drive through.

"When in Rome..." Fr. Louis smiled an impish grin and reached for the bat in Fr. Malcolm's hand. The thrill of playing his only game of baseball, in Italy of all places, suddenly filled the slightly inebriated priest with visions of past glory when he got the game-winning hit and was wildly congratulated by the American seminarians studying with him at the Gregorian.

"Let's go," Fr. Malcolm said and hurried onto the dimly lit field, the couple of lights sufficiently illuminating their play on the perfectly manicured grass.

"C'mon, Louis, keep your eye on the ball," Fr. Regis said as his friend swung through the slow-pitched softball again.

"*Une de plus*," Fr. Louis said, determined to hit it over the head of Fr. Malcolm who had moved in to play a shallow shortstop. He unzipped his jacket to free up his swing.

Thwack! Fr. Louis hit the pitched ball over the outstretched arm of Fr. Malcolm into centerfield and ran to first base, or about where first base would have been if there had been bases on the field. With Fr. Malcolm chasing the ball in the outfield, Fr. Louis curved past where second base would have been as Fr. Regis moved over to cover third.

"Throw it, Malcolm," Fr. Regis called out to his friend with the speedy Fr. Louis bearing down on him.

And all Fr. Louis could hear was his father's voice recounting the great Roberto galloping around second base, running out from under his cap and sliding into third base on one of his storied triples. So Fr. Louis half-slid, half-rolled toward where Fr. Regis stood at the baseline, ahead of Fr. Malcolm's throw, the softball glancing off his back.

"Take it easy," Fr. Regis said. "You'll break something."

Fr. Louis got up to dust off his pants, noticing the hole in his dark trousers at the knee.

"Way to go, Big Lou," Fr. Malcolm said, trotting into the infield, having lost his cigar somewhere in the outfield grass.

"Having fun, boys?" They heard a man's voice say facetiously before they saw the young policeman, about their age, standing near home plate. "Didn't you read the sign: 'No trespassing after dark'?"

The three of them stood silently in the vicinity of third base.

"We didn't see any signs, officer," Fr. Malcolm said, trying to hide his ponytail beneath his jacket collar. "Honest."

"Ah-hunh," the deputy said as he approached them. "Who are you all? A little past your prime for these shenanigans, wouldn't you say?"

"We're on a pilgrimage to the Shrine of the North American Martyrs in Auriesville tomorrow," Fr. Louis said. "We stopped here to tour the Hall of Fame."

"Say what?" the deputy said as the waft of alcohol from their close breaths came to him unmistakably. "Had a few, hunh?"

"We had supper at Bambino's," Fr. Regis said, hoping to establish some good will. "You know, a couple beers and wine with our meal."

"Don't say," the deputy said. "Is that Jeep over there one of yours? The one with the Pennsylvania plate parked in front of the 'No trespassing' sign."

"It's mine," Fr. Malcolm said. "I didn't see the sign."

"I'll bet you didn't," the officer said. "I ran the plate...we'll see in a minute."

Just then, a scratchy voice broke in on his walkie-talkie and the deputy held the device close to his face. "Merle here, Chief."

"Merle, this is Chief Matthews. I have the plate for you."

"Go ahead, Chief," the deputy said. "I'm here with the three all-stars in Doubleday." He couldn't keep himself from snickering.

"The Chief says it's registered to a Malcolm O'Shea of Tionesta." The deputy looked them over. "Which one of you is him, and do you have the owner's card?"

"It's in the glove compartment with my insurance card," Fr. Malcolm said, handing the deputy his car keys.

"That's convenient." The deputy tried to sound officious but he was having too much fun. "License?"

"It's in the motel with my wallet," Fr. Malcolm said.

"We're staying in the Lakeside Motel on First Street," Fr. Regis said, trying to establish their legitimacy.

"So you went to the restaurant with no money or credit cards?" The deputy tried to investigate a little further; but he could tell they were harmless.

"Well, I have money, sir," Fr. Louis said. "I won it gambling."

"Gambling?" The deputy tried to sound indignant. "Maybe we should go down the station."

"Is that necessary, officer? We stopped at the Indian casino outside of Rome," Fr. Regis explained.

"Where?" he said, genuinely confused.

"Rome, New York, off of I-90," Fr. Malcolm said, trying to be helpful.

"We were just having a little fun recalling our days studying for the ministry together at the North American College." Fr. Regis used the trump card hoping to avoid being taken to the police station.

"Well, well," an older man's voice came to them out of the darkness. "What do we have here, Deputy Merle? The Three Musketeers?"

"More like the Three Stooges, I'd say," the deputy said. "They say they're ministers on some kind of trip to a shrine or something."

"The North American Martyrs Shrine in Auriesville," Fr. Regis said. "It's the same name of the seminary we studied at in Rome."

"New York?" The deputy said.

"Italy," Fr. Malcolm said.

The chief seemed to bristle with the mention of that ancient city. "You Catholic priests?"

"Yes, sir," Fr. Louis said, accustomed to the cooperation he enjoyed with the officialdom in Montreal.

"That's the one said he won a lot of money gambling," the deputy said.

"Let's take a ride to the station, boys, and sort all of this out," the chief said. "You two come with me. Merle take the big one. Turn around; we have to cuff you, you know."

"Is this necessary?" Fr. Regis asked.

"Procedure," the police chief said. "You can appreciate rules and all, Fathers, can't you? We may have to impound the vehicle, too. We'll see."

So, as Fr. Louis and Fr. Regis got into the back seat of the chief's patrol car, Fr. Malcolm slid into the back seat of the deputy's. Driving quietly the few blocks to the police station, Chief Matthews began to pray silently for the first time in more than a year.

Lord, you have delivered these Romish priests into my hands, he began in silent glee. *And like Elijah on Mt. Tabor, I will smote these hocus-pocus wizards for your glory. And if I have a little fun in the smotin', so be it. The Good Book says it is a terrible thing to be delivered into the hands of the living God.* He surprised himself with the scripture verses he had learned in Sunday school that suddenly came to mind. *After all*, he continued his disingenuous prayer, *they won't be burned up in a blaze of fire, anyhow,*

*just twitching in guilt while they lose a night's
sleep in my jail. Amen.*

He pulled his patrol car in front of the police
station on Main Street with the deputy behind
him. They led the three priests into the station
house, shackled and somber like some ritual
sheep being led to slaughter.

"You can enjoy our accommodations while
we sort out this situation, reverend fathers,"
Chief Matthews said sarcastically as he took off
the handcuffs. Fr. Malcolm joined them in the
holding cell.

"Did the magistrate go on that hunting trip
to Canada with Russell and the guys?" the
Chief asked his deputy.

"Yeah, I think so," the deputy said. "They
won't be back until Thursday night."

"I am from Canada," Fr. Louis volunteered.
"Montreal."

"Don't say." The Chief eyed him suspiciously. "This gets more intriguing by the minute, Merle."

The two peace officers returned to the front office, leaving the three pilgrim priests in the jail cell to fret about their predicament.

"What do you want to do with them, Chief?" the deputy said. "They're priests 'n' all."

"Liquored priests trespassing on an American institution that we are solemnly charged to protect," he reminded his deputy. "Now, I can see they're harmless as children; but, the fact remains, they broke the law and I mean to teach them a lesson. If a night in jail is what it takes to uphold the order in Cooperstown, then so be it, even if we drop the charges in the morning."

"I guess so," the deputy said. "But all they were doing was playing a little ball after dark like a dozen other times we've run guys off."

"Nonetheless," the chief said curtly. "Go down the Lakeside Motel and talk with Harold to see if their story checks out. He'll have a copy of the license."

When the deputy left the station, the chief took to meditating on the situation again, and his quiet prayer rose in the approximate direction of heaven as he leaned back in his swivel chair with his feet propped up on the desk and his hands across his belly.

Lord, he began, *it'll serve that woman right for making me take our children to that Church every Sunday when I would just as soon attend to my duties, or occasionally fish the Susquehanna for some peace and quiet. Why I ever agreed to raise our darlings Catholic I'll never understand; I don't hardly remember promising it, anyhow. It had to be that I was under that woman's spell of beauty that must've made my brain soft and let her baptize our babies in St. Mary's Church rather than the Main Street Baptist Church like I was when I came of age.*

He got up and poured himself a cup of stale, bitter coffee. He looked at the wall clock—9:16 —momentarily thinking it was a pertinent scripture verse, but he couldn't recollect the reference. He sat down in his swivel chair at his big desk and continued his lamentation. *You can see, Lord, why I'm feeling vindicated here, why if I have a little sport with these three priests, it's only in retribution for the hundreds of times that I have had to sit through all that getting up and kneeling down and unfamiliar mumbled prayers when, You know as well as I that I shouldn't be kneeling on this bad knee at all since I sprained it at the Church picnic playing in that father-son softball game last year.* He paused to recall his place at prayer. *So, even if we have run off dozens of would-be hall-of-famers without detaining them, You can see that I am just taking fair advantage of the scales of justice,*

*as my position and your Good Book allows.
Amen, I think.*

As they sobered up in the cramped jail cell,
with the gray ceiling paint cracked and peeling
above them, the three priests worried about
their predicament, realizing that an arrest
could cause scandal for their dioceses, even
something as innocuous as playing baseball on
Doubleday Field after dark while under the in-
fluence of alcohol. They wouldn't allow themselves to whisper their worst fears to each
other, so anxious were they with their plight.
Fr. Regis, who knew about these things from
his work in the chancery, dreaded having to go
to some priest's rehabilitation center, where he
would be examined by psychologists to deter-
mine his sobriety. Fr. Malcolm feared the diocese would find him an assignment even more
remote than the heart of the national forest,
where his name could be tactfully forgotten.
Fr. Louis, his lowered head in his hands, anx-

iously wondered how he could ever explain an arrest for playing baseball to his bishop, let alone gambling, when he was supposed to be on a pilgrimage in the United States.

"I wonder what your bishops would think if they knew their men were arrested for public intoxication, trespassing, and disorderly conduct," Chief Matthews said as he came by to check on his prisoners—though he disliked Catholic bishops even more than priests.

The three priests were too humiliated to offer even a feeble defense of their actions. They felt like they were doomed to suffer the consequences of their reckless behavior.

"It was my idea, sir," Fr. Malcolm finally said. "I talked them into it—my gloves, bat, and ball."

"Well, that's right noble of you, son," the chief said. "But all of you were trespassing on Doubleday. We have to protect it for historical purposes. Do you have any idea how many would-be Joe DiMaggios try to water that grass each year? At least you three were trying to play ball. Otherwise you'd be looking at public indecency, too."

The faces of the three priests blanched at the thought of such a charge being reported to their bishops.

"We're really sorry," Fr. Regis pleaded. "It will never happen again."

"I should hope not," Chief Matthews said and couldn't help but delight in the turnabout of these three priests confessing their sins and seeking his forgiveness. Then the thought of his wife, Theresa, finding out how he was toying with the priests filled him with a sudden, dark dread about just how miserable she could make his life, and for how long.

"Is there a fine we could pay?" Fr. Louis offered.

"Are you trying to bribe an officer of the law?" Chief Matthews said with indignation. "I don't know how they do things up in Canada, but in Cooperstown justice is not for sale."

"No, no," Fr. Louis said. "A donation to a charity or something like that."

"Chief," the deputy said as he joined them. "There is the Thanksgiving community supper coming up at the lodge next month."

"Are you daft, too?" the chief said. "Even if we drop all the charges, if I said, there can't be no *quid pro quo*—see, I know some Latin, too," and turned to the jailed priests.

"But if you did let us go," Fr. Regis reasoned aloud at this first glimmer of hope. "And we were to make a free will offering in support of that supper, then there would be no *quid pro quo*—just a donation in support of the good people of Cooperstown for Thanksgiving, a national holiday."

"How would Judge Taylor look at that, though?" the chief speculated aloud.

"He'd be happy you found someone else to buy the turkeys," the deputy declared.

"That's a fact," the chief said. He dreaded having to explain to his wife why he had charged the priests for playing baseball after hours, let alone keeping them in jail overnight. He motioned to his deputy to join him in the front office.

"Everything checked out at the motel," the deputy reported. "They're who they say they are. The car is clean; no outstandings."

Looking at the clock, again, Chief Matthews resigned himself to his wife's omnipresence and strong Catholic faith. "I'm going home now, Merle," he said. "Before Theresa puts the kids to bed. Make them some fresh coffee and give them some of her blueberry muffins from the other day. That'll help sober them up. Let them go at first light. But don't tell them until the morning. A little purgation will do them good," he snickered, amused with his Catholic joke at the priests' expense.

"Hunh?" Merle said. "What about the turkeys?"

"Don't take one penny from them, you hear?" Chief Matthews said and poked his deputy's badge. "I'm not losing my pension over some turkeys, let alone some Catholic priests. Not a penny. And not a word to Theresa," the chief said before he went out of the door. "Not a word."

The deputy made a new pot of coffee and found the plastic container with the muffins. Uneasy with jailing the priests overnight, he was happy to make amends with some small-town hospitality.

Once the coffee was ready, Deputy Merle put the pot on the tray with the cups, sugar, creamer, and some napkins and stirrers. He carried the tray into the priests with one hand and pulled open the unlocked cell door with the other. "Here," he set the tray on one of the four cots. "The Chief's wife made the muffins; they're good."

"Thank you," the priests said. "Thanks."

"It'll be all right," the deputy said as he closed the unlocked cell door behind him. "Goodnight, I'll be out here if you need anything; the bathroom's at the end of the hall."

"Goodnight," they said.

"You mean that's been unlocked the whole time?" Fr. Malcolm said.

"What? Are you going to break out and go underground now," Fr. Regis said.

"Looks like God sent us an angel of mercy," Fr. Louis said and poured the hot coffee. "Do you think they're going to let us go in the morning?"

"What did he say?" Fr. Malcolm asked.

"'It'll be all right.'" Fr. Regis repeated the deputy's vague reassurance.

"Coffee's good," Fr. Louis said and took another sip.

"The muffins are good, too," Fr. Malcolm said, devouring one in a couple of bites.

"Here we are," Fr. Regis said. "Eating again."

They dared to laugh together, but not too loud, the coffee and muffins beginning to blunt the effects of the wine and beer. Finishing the food and drink, they were just sleepy now, welcoming their repose on the hard cell cots. Under the sympathetic eye of the kind deputy, the three priests dreamt away their fears, daring to hope for release from their inconvenient incarceration like some apostolic heroes freed from their prison chains.

Third Day

"Rise and shine," Deputy Merle said.

The three priests stirred with the greeting of the peace officer and the sharp sound of the door clanging open. The faint dawn light brightened their small jail cell. Their heads were still a little dull and slow from the alcohol and their ordeal, as they woke from their restless sleep in the Cooperstown police station.

"The chief says we're dropping all the charges." The deputy handed the car keys to Fr. Malcolm as the three of them stood silently in the dingy office. "You're free to go and continue your—whatever."

"Pilgrimage," Fr. Regis said,

"Pilgrimage," the deputy echoed, happy to be letting the priests walk out of jail with some semblance of religious tolerance established. "Don't forget your stuff," the deputy said, handing them the gloves, bat, and ball from his desk.

"*Merci*," Fr. Louis said as he took the ball.

"Thank you," Fr. Malcolm said as he slid the bat handle inside the opening on the backside of his gloves.

"Tell the chief we're much obliged," Fr. Regis said as he opened the door to the promise of the cool morning's light.

Fr. Malcolm grunted something about "getting the Jeep," feeling guilty for having been the cause of their night's travail. Without saying much, Fathers Regis and Louis started walking toward their motel, with Fr. Louis tossing the ball into the air a couple of feet and catching it as they continued on the quiet sidewalk past the closed store fronts.

The misadventure had drawn the three friends closer together, like when they were traveling in Europe during their years in the seminary; and now their groggy heads seemed to be thinking the same thing: Let's get out of town as soon as possible. By the time Fr. Regis and Fr. Louis had freshened up and changed into their blacks, Fr. Malcolm had parked his Jeep in front of the motel office. He met Fr. Regis in the doorway of their room and told him he would be just a few minutes packing his suitcase. Meanwhile, Fr. Louis went to the office to turn in his room key and settle any additional charges on their motel bill with his winnings from the Oneida casino. In a few minutes, they were throwing their bags into the back of the Cherokee and pulling out of the motel parking lot. They were anxious to get out of Cooperstown.

Fr. Malcolm drove carefully, slowly, noticing a patrol car in his rear view mirror escorting them to the edge of town, Chief Matthews waving farewell to the three clerics as they turned onto the state road, his final and ironic tribute to his wife's Catholic faith.

"Can we make a donation?" Fr. Malcolm mocked Fr. Louis once they were a few minutes north of town on S.R. 80, with the windows opened to the fresh morning air, and headed for the interstate highway.

They all laughed, releasing the tension that had constrained their frivolity for the past dozen hours or so. Recounting their ordeal at the mercy of the police chief, they alternated between laughter and complaints, retelling their misadventure and speculating about the repercussions if they had been formally charged.

"I think he had something against Catholics," Fr. Louis said naively, inciting them to another round of laughter.

Returning to Interstate 90, the central corridor of their pilgrimage, the morning's light illumined the highway and emboldened their accounts as they retold and exaggerated their encounter with small-town justice. For, after all, they were good priests and this was as close as any of them had come to getting in trouble with the law since they were detained at the border of Croatia and Bosnia-Herzegovina over a dozen years earlier on their trip to Medjugorje. And, like all Catholic clergy over the past twenty years or so, they dreaded any association with scandal, seeing as the Church had more than her share during their lifetime. Some morning traffic accompanied them on the highway, including a dozen motorcycles whizzing past the Jeep.

"I need some coffee," Fr. Regis said. "Auriesville is less than twenty-five miles from here."

"I'm hungry," Fr. Malcolm said. "Let's get some breakfast."

"*Oui,*" Fr. Louis muttered his concurrence. "*J'ai faime.*"

They stopped at the next exit advertising food and gas. The hearty breakfast, the excited chatter over the ample coffee, and the familiarity of a diner's table helped them to clear their heads and put the close memory of Cooperstown behind them. After breakfast, Fr. Malcolm filled his tank at the nearby gas station.

Driving the last several miles to the shrine site, they began to quietly prepare for the celebration of Mass on this Feast of the North American Martyrs that was the purpose and destination of this October pilgrimage in the first place. Like those earlier disciples freed by angelic messengers from their incarceration, the three priests tried to set their hearts on the spiritual duty that lay before them. Pulling into the large parking lot, they felt united, not only by their ordeal, but also by that fraternal bond first formed at the American theologate in Rome named after these same French martyrs, and later intensified by their ordinations to the priesthood of Jesus Christ.

The lot was partially filled with buses and cars carrying pilgrims from throughout the region to the shrine on this day of solemn celebration. Fr. Malcolm parked the Jeep as near to the road as possible. The priests gathered their garment bags holding their albs from the back of the Jeep. A light breeze swirled above the Mohawk River Valley as they walked past the Visitor's Center and crossed the road onto the main property, where hundreds of adults and children moved freely between the various chapels and crosses, statues and stations, gardens and memorials.

"I've never been here before," Fr. Louis said as he surveyed the hundreds of acres comprising the shrine site. "It's rustic, yet venerable."

The three priests continued walking toward the large, round church built in 1903 and reminiscent of the Roman Colosseum. Their Mass was scheduled for twelve noon.

"We can take a better look at everything after Mass," Fr. Regis said, cognizant of the twenty minutes they had to vest, prepare, and set up for the sacred mysteries.

Entering the circular church, Fr. Regis led the others down a long descending aisle and then up a few steps to the sacristy in the center of the four altars facing north, east, south and west. Hundreds of people were in the church, some sitting, others walking around, a few praying quietly. A Mass was finishing on one of the other altars, the last communicant returning to the long benches that served as pews. They hung their clothing bags on the hooks in the small sacristy. The red stoles and chasubles for their afternoon Mass were set out neatly on three hangers. The three priests waited until the priest who had just finished liturgy had taken off his vestments before they began to put theirs on over their albs in the small sacristy. When the other priest left, the sacristan brought the vessels and chalice into the sacristy to prepare them for the next Mass.

"Who's the principal celebrant?" the sacristan asked quickly.

"I am," Fr. Malcolm said, a little self-conscious that he was the only one of them not in clerical clothes and collar.

The sacristan glanced at Fr. Malcolm and then continued filling the cruets with wine and water, the ciborium with hosts, and getting fresh linens from a drawer. Placing the chalice and vessels on a tray, he turned to the priests as he neared the curtained doorway. "Please sign the registry and place your *celebrets* on the counter."

Fr. Regis and Fr. Louis dutifully pulled their temporary identification cards from their wallets and placed them on the countertop. Fr. Malcolm was signing the registry when his face went white as he realized he had forgotten to obtain the needed *celebret* for a visiting priest; he had developed the habit of avoiding calling his chancery over the past couple of years unless it was an emergency. The others stared at him, shaking their heads disapprovingly. The shrine church, like so many places across the country since the scandals, had become strict

195

about priests demonstrating their good standing.

"Put the chasuble on," Fr. Regis whispered to Fr. Malcolm. He handed one of the bright matching stoles to Fr. Louis. "I'll do the reading, Louis. You can do the petitions."

"We'll be starting in a couple of minutes." Fr. Louis pointed to the clock that hung beneath the crucifix in the sacristy.

"We can all distribute communion," Fr. Regis said, recalling the other times he had celebrated Mass at the shrine. "There'll be a crowd for the noon Mass on the feast day."

Fr. Malcolm, Fr. Regis, and Fr. Louis peeked out from behind the black curtain veiling the sacristy entrance and saw the large crowd of pilgrims, maybe 700, or so. Then they noticed the sacristan helping a woman who seemed to have stumbled. The sacristan glanced back toward them as the noon bell sounded, motioning to start Mass with a slight rolling of his free hand.

"Better to ask forgiveness than permission," Fr. Regis whispered to Fr. Malcolm in reference to the forgotten *celebret*. "Ring the bell, Louis."

Fr. Louis pulled the short rope that rang the little bell hanging on the door frame. As the three priests walked out into the sanctuary, the people stood and sang a couple of *a cappella* verses of "Faith of our Fathers," the familiar Catholic hymn appropriate for the martyrs' feast day.

As the three friends bowed to the altar and then genuflected before the tabernacle housing the Lord, they knew that this Mass was the anticipated climax of their pilgrimage. It was almost as if the night's incarceration was the small price they had to pay for the privilege of celebrating this liturgy.

Fr. Malcolm made the sign of the cross on his body, intoning the Trinitarian name of God: "In the name of the Father, and of the Son, and of the Holy Spirit." Simultaneously, the other priests and all of the people, adults and children, blessed themselves and, with that, were enveloped in the sacred mysteries. Looking out into the pious faces of the other pilgrims, Fr. Malcolm was sensitive to their corporate identity in Christ, extending his arms in welcome, invoking the grace, love, and fellowship of the Holy Trinity in his deep, resonant voice. His dark eyes welled up with tears momentarily as he prayed the Penitential Rite, beseeching God's mercy on all of their souls, especially his own. The guilt of his attraction to Leah felt like a burning weight in his chest as he asked the Lord's mercy. The chanted Gloria rose in rhythmic waves, filling the cavernous Church, calling dozens of other visitors to noon Mass. Through the scripture readings and psalm response, Fr. Malcolm tried to keep his composure, gathering himself for the homily.

And it was with his rambling sermon that he was changed in some ethereal and numinous way. By the time he began preaching, there were nearly one thousand people listening for the Spirit's animation of this tall ponytailed priest, whose native bloodline, unknown to them, had been on the wrong side of these martyrs' deaths. The Holy Spirit did not disappoint them, enlivening the young priest's every word, Fr. Malcolm glancing at his note cards only once to be certain to articulate the French names of those heroic Jesuit missionaries: St. Isaac Jogues, St. Rene Goupil, and St. John Lalande.

In his homily, Fr. Malcolm kept coming back to the theme: the cost of discipleship. As he preached about the martyrs' courageous witness, he tried to recall the theological source for his central message, but the name or title eluded him. And while he held the hundreds of pilgrims rapt and leaning towards him like children drawn to a campfire, there was another and ironic sermon playing out in his conscience, juxtaposing the martyrs' sacrifice with his own indulgent attraction for Leah. The power of his words seemed to unravel the tension within him, releasing that contortion of faith and doubt, his vow of celibacy and his temptation. Listening to their friend's unusually poignant oration, Fr. Regis and Fr. Louis noted the passionate conviction with which he spoke, his long arms waving out for emphasis, the inked eagle's claw flashing beneath the billowing folds of his crimson chasuble as he recounted the story of the martyrs' willing return to this place of pain and sorrow. After about twenty minutes, he wound down, his face flushed with color, his closing phrase resonating above the pilgrim congregation with a kind of faint echo that embedded the words into their mind and memory: "The blood of these martyrs was the seed of faith sown in the New World."

When he finally sat down following the proclamation of the Creed and Fr. Louis' praying the petitions, Fr. Malcolm was almost trembling, the tingling in his limbs releasing the pressure that had tensed his body while he spoke from the pulpit. He welcomed the few minutes the ushers took to take up the collection in support of the shrine, needing the time to get his liturgical bearings.

For the remainder of Mass, Fr. Malcolm proceeded with a quiet solemnity through the chants and responses that framed the Eucharistic prayer, the lone wail of an innocent babe giving veiled voice to the martyrs' memory. The three priests distributed communion to the nearly one thousand pilgrims, while a young woman played some soft hymns on the organ in the chamber at the center of the four altars. After the closing Trinitarian blessing, the priests kissed the altar and returned to the sacristy.

As they removed their vestments and albs, they looked at each other in silence for a few moments.

"What was that?" Fr. Regis asked Fr. Malcolm.

"Have you been reading Bonhoeffer?" Fr. Louis asked.

"Bonhoeffer?" Fr. Malcolm whispered. "Not since the seminary."

"I never heard you preach like that," Fr. Regis said.

"Passionate and eloquent," Fr. Louis said. "You had them in the palm of your hand."

"I don't know what got into me," Fr. Malcolm said, but he intuited that the homily had resolved his conflict somehow, that this feast of martyrs had graced the moral dilemma over his attraction to Leah, and that he had come out on the other side, free, and with his vow intact. "I guess this place got to me."

"Don't forget to take your *celebrets*," the sacristan said as he came into the sacristy with the chalice and vessels. "Father, that was one of the best homilies I ever heard about the martyrs," he said to Fr. Malcolm. "And I've heard my share of them these past dozen years."

"Thank you," Fr. Malcolm said, happy that the issue of his forgotten *celebret* appeared to be forgotten with the celebration of the sacred mysteries.

Fr. Louis put a fifty dollar bill in the envelope near the registration book in support of the shrine. When he shook hands with the sacristan, he slipped another folded fifty into his palm.

"Thanks," the sacristan said. "Where are you from?"

"I'm from Montreal," he said. "Fr. Regis is from Buffalo, and Fr. Malcolm is from Pennsylvania. This is the final day of our pilgrimage."

"We studied together in Rome back in the day," Fr. Regis said and shook the sacristan's hand.

"And what's your name?" Fr. Malcolm asked.

"William," the sacristan answered. "I'm a lay associate of the Jesuit community here in Auriesville."

"Thanks for your help," Fr. Malcolm said.

The priests gathered their garment bags and walked through the large Church. People were still lingering after Mass, lighting candles, whispering prayers.

"I think there's a few hundred acres on the shrine site," Fr. Regis said as they started walking on the expansive grounds.

"Do you know where the bodies are buried?" Fr. Louis asked. "I didn't see any reliquaries in the pamphlet."

"They never recovered the bodies." Fr. Regis directed them to a monument dedicated to the unborn overlooking the river valley. "They were killed in the ravine on the other side where we parked."

"They were tortured, dismembered, their bodies left for animals," Fr. Malcolm explained. "Then, whatever was left was thrown into the river."

"St. John de Brebeuf and our other four martyrs were all Jesuit priests," Fr. Louis said, shifting his garment bag onto his other arm.

"Isaac Jogues was a priest," Fr. Malcolm said. "The other two were oblates: Rene Goupil a doctor and John Lalande a volunteer missionary."

"There's a lot of people here today," Fr. Regis said, enjoying the beauty of the winding Mohawk River valley. "Let's put these albs in the car and grab something quick to eat at the Visitor's Center."

205

"Yeah," Fr. Malcolm said. "A sandwich or something."

"There's a gift shop there, too," Fr. Louis said. "I can buy something for *ma mère*."

Walking across the grounds of the shrine, they greeted random pilgrims and a large group of school children. After they put their garment bags in the Jeep, they found a corner table in the cafeteria and had a simple lunch of sandwiches, sodas, and chips. They talked about their priestly lives, their work, their struggles, the noise of the crowd insulating their confidential exchange from the families and school children enjoying their lunches, too. Occasionally, the priests smiled or waved at the people greeting them as they walked by with their trays. Then, Fr. Regis' cell phone emitted a low buzz and vibration. "I have to take this; it's him." Fr. Regis got up and walked out of the cafeteria as he began his conversation with the bishop. When he returned to their table after a few minutes, he was agitated.

"Another emergency," Fr. Regis said. "When I get back I have to negotiate a parish closing—some of the people locked themselves in the church to protest. It was on the noon news. He's worked up, too, because it's the last Slovenian parish in the diocese; his grandmother was Slovenian."

The two friends knew he was talking about his bishop, though he tactfully avoided using his name in this public space. It was a code they had grown accustomed to the past couple of days whenever he went off on one of his diocesan diatribes. They let him vent his frustrations at lunch as they had throughout the pilgrimage, realizing that their friend needed to unburden himself to a sympathetic audience.

"I'm sorry for beating your ears, again," Fr. Regis said. "But who else can I tell this stuff to?"

"Do you guys want to go to Blessed Kateri Tekakwitha's Shrine?" Fr. Malcolm asked, hoping to change the conversation. "I'd like to see that new Indian Museum that they established when they remodeled the shrine a few years ago."

"Is it far?" Fr. Louis asked.

"No," Fr. Regis said. "It's just across the river valley on the other side of the highway in Fonda—fifteen minutes or so."

"There's a Canadian shrine to Blessed Kateri at an Indian village outside of Montreal," Fr. Louis said. "I've taken some diocesan pilgrimages there over the years in anticipation of her canonization. She could be canonized next year."

"They'll be open for a couple of hours yet," Fr. Malcolm said. "We have plenty of time."

"Let me make a quick stop at the gift shop for *ma mère*," Fr. Louis said.

Fr. Louis bought his mother a beautiful set of amethyst rosary beads at the gift shop to suit the color of her eyes. *She was the one who taught me to pray the rosary with our family after supper*, he thought, carefully placing the box in his suitcase when they returned to Malcolm's Jeep. *I could use a couple of rosaries now*, he mused as they pulled out of the parking lot

During the short ride to the Tekakwitha Shrine, Fr. Malcolm explained that the site had been remodeled in 2002 because she was designated the Patroness of World Youth Day that was being held in Toronto that year. "The diocese figured that there would be a lot of young people passing through on their way to Canada," he said. "So they put some money into the place. It was long overdue."

"Here we are." Fr. Malcolm pulled his Jeep Cherokee into the parking lot of the shrine. There were several other cars scattered around the lot.

"Those stations look new," Fr. Regis said and pointed to one of the large, carved Stations of the Cross on the perimeter of the grounds as they got out of the Jeep. "I was here a few years before the renovation."

They walked into the visitors' building, curious to explore this smaller site dedicated to the Lily of the Mohawks. Fr. Malcolm asked the woman at the counter where the Native American Museum was located and she directed him outside to St. Peter's Chapel, where it was situated beneath the church. Fr. Regis and Fr. Louis meandered through the gift shop, noticing the contrast between the locally made religious items and the mass-produced ones available in most shrine shops or Catholic religious catalogues.

"I thought she was born in Auriesville?" Fr. Louis asked Fr. Regis, who was holding a colorful beaded belt.

"She was," he said. "But the original village was burned down by your French Canadians when she was an adolescent and they moved here for safety with the other Mohawks."

"I think Pope Benedict is supposed to canonize her next year," Fr. Regis said. "I've heard the ecclesiastical rumors."

"Look at this," Fr. Louis said, holding up a flat, handcrafted crucifix with a picture story of Blessed Kateri's life colorfully etched into the wood of the cross like a totem around the corpus of Christ. "That's different."

"How much is it?" Fr. Regis asked.

"One-hundred-twenty-five dollars," Fr. Louis read the price tag.

"I'm going to buy it." Fr. Regis admired the large, colorful crucifix. "I'll give it to the bishop as a kind of peace offering for all the complaining I did about him during the trip."

They both laughed, releasing the tension that had accompanied any reference to the bishop the past three days.

"That was made by a local Indian artist," the kind, bespectacled woman at the counter said as she rang up the purchase. "We've sold a few of them this year."

"It's beautiful," Fr. Regis said, pleased with the conciliatory artifact he had purchased for his maligned bishop.

"How long is the shrine open today?" Fr. Louis asked.

"Until four o'clock. You have about an hour or so," she said, glancing at the clock behind her. "Thank you."

The two priests walked outside to the nearby St. Peter Chapel. They felt the slight autumn chill in the late afternoon air.

"I'm going to catch up with Malcolm in the museum," Fr. Regis said.

"I think I'll just pray awhile," Fr. Louis said and went into the empty chapel. It was like hundreds of other churches that he had visited over the years in the Americas, Europe, and the Middle East, only smaller. He genuflected to the presence of Christ in the tabernacle. He sat in a pew in the middle of the church and closed his eyes. He took a couple of deep breaths and asked the Holy Spirit to inspire his prayer. The faint smell of incense lingering from the midday Mass of the martyrs came to him like a familiar reassurance. Then he sensed a kind of subtle presence permeating the dimly lit chapel, an awareness of God in and around him, filling his soul. His ears seemed to ring slightly in the silence. Tears fell from his blue eyes; he could almost hear his heartbeat. Opening his eyes he peered toward the tabernacle behind the altar and whispered a simple prayer in the name to whom he had vowed his life: "Jesus," he prayed. "Jesus." He sat motionless for quite a while, oblivious to the chapel door opening and closing, basking in the peace of God's grace that enveloped him like an embrace. He knew his year of aridity had ended, the precious consolation a privileged gift from the Lord. He savored the dulling of his senses, his soul aflame with love.

"Excuse me, Father," the custodian said softly. "We're closing up, now—Father?"

Fr. Louis smiled and nodded to the old man as he got up, careful to genuflect his fidelity. As he stepped out of the chapel, the cool air seemed to tickle his face and hands, the day's light diffused and fading. He saw his two friends talking by the Jeep and he walked down the steps to join them.

"We were going to leave you here," Fr. Regis teased him. "But then we remembered that you're buying the last supper of the pilgrimage, so we thought we'd wait."

"I'm ready to go now," Fr. Louis said, still a little distracted. He climbed into the back seat of Fr. Malcolm's Jeep.

"You should've seen that museum, Lou," Fr. Malcolm started as they pulled out of the parking lot. "I picked up a book about Hiawatha and the Iroquois Confederation. Did you know that Benjamin Franklin used that as his model in persuading the colonies to unite against English rule?"

"Who's Benjamin Franklin?" Fr. Louis, recovering from his disorientation, teased his earnest friend.

"Wise guy," Fr. Malcolm said.

"We had a chance to see the archeological excavation of the old village, too," Fr. Regis said. "While you were in there praying."

"It was the site of the original chapel," Fr. Malcolm said.

"Malcolm, let's take the scenic ride along Route 5," Fr. Regis said. "It meanders with the river all the way to Utica. It'll be beautiful this time of year."

"That sounds good to me," Fr. Louis offered.

"The entrance to Route 5 is right up here a ways," Fr. Regis said. "Past the signs to I-90."

"I'm game," Fr. Malcolm said.

"I think the World Series starts tonight," Fr. Regis said. "We'll get back in time to catch the last few innings on TV."

"Are the Pittsburgh Pirates playing?" Fr. Louis asked.

"No—they haven't won in twenty years," Fr. Malcolm said.

"It's the Texas Rangers versus the St. Louis Cardinals," Fr. Regis said.

"I'm not rooting for some cowboys," Fr. Louis joked. "I'll take my sainted namesake and the hierarchy—that sounds like a winner to me."

"Birds, not bishops," Fr. Malcolm said, shaking his head in mock disgust. "Canadians." He turned the Jeep onto the state road that paralleled the meandering Mohawk. Immediately, they were immersed in the tranquil beauty of the river valley.

"*C'est magnifique,*" Fr. Louis said as they drove along the ambling course of the Mohawk River winding through the colorful autumn hills of the valley, that deep peace still pulsing in his heart.

"Regis, as a priest, if I instruct someone in the RCIA can I be her sponsor for Confirmation at the Cathedral with the bishop?" Fr. Malcolm asked, the last prick at his conscience causing him to clarify his relationship with Leah, aloud.

"Sure, you can," Fr. Regis said. "Why not?"

"Unless you've fallen in love with some Indian maiden?" Fr. Louis teased his friend, oblivious to how close to the bone his words had cut.

Fr. Malcolm's face flushed with shame for a moment, unnoticed by his friends. He chuckled self-consciously to hide his embarrassment. Then, he sighed, thankful that Fr. Louis' inadvertent insight freed him from disclosing his near indiscretion to his classmates.

"You guys have to listen to this," he said, quick to divert attention away from himself. He reached up for the compact disc he had clipped to the visor above his head and then inserted it into the CD player. "This was written by St. John de Brebeuf from the original Huron. I was waiting for the right moment to play it on the pilgrimage."

So, they drove westward on State Road 5 rolling along the Mohawk River, the haunting chant rising from the car's speakers in that forgotten tongue of a native people long defeated and dispersed, the words unintelligible to them save the "Yesus" whose birth the song proclaimed. The primitive, rhythmic drums resounded through the swerving Jeep as the Huron chant, the fresh October air, the reds, yellows, and oranges of the valley, and the smell of the river coalesced into a kind of synergy of their senses. Mindful of the martyrs' blood that watered those ancient hills, the priests drove as if crossing some frontier of rich autumn hues in pursuit of that fierce and elusive holiness vaguely intuited in their Christian bones, drawn by the relentless mercy of God working in all these things for the good of those who love Him.

PROMISE

Oogae said, "The cold? It's always a consideration," in that concluding tone of his, that voice that stopped the wandering and peeking of the conversation, drew nods and settled everything, without answer. Humbert Biitner, known as Oogae for the past thirty-some years, got up. He walked over to the curb, patted his big, round belly, and spat into the street. Behind him on the pavement the men knew it was time to go home.

"Well, whaddaya think?" one of the men said looking across at the two- and three-story rowhouses, typical of Pittsburgh neighborhoods.

"Yeah, I guess you're right." Another got up and folded his aluminum lawn chair. The other men in front of the shoemaker's shop folded their chairs too.

"I'll betcha it's past midnight?"

"No foolin'."

"Twelve twenty-five."

"Naw, twelve forty-five." Vic's fixed face widened into a yawn and he looked up and down Forbes Avenue, squinting his eyes, as if a panorama of the neighborhood would verify the suspected time.

"A buck says twelve-thirty on the nose. Oogae?"

Turning toward his friends, Humbert Biitner snapped his left arm out to draw back the shirt cuff and expose his silver wristwatch.

221

Slowly, he brought his hand near to his face, where, with the cast of the streetlight, he could see the small black numbers. "Twelve thirty-five," Oogae said in that certain voice that they wanted to hear. Oogae walked over to his wooden folding chair and snapped it shut. Already, some were straggling away, down the avenue, chairs under their arms.

"Good night. See ya, Oogae."

"See ya tomorra?" With that, another went in the other direction along Forbes toward his house, two blocks away.

Oogae watched Vic dart between two parked cars to avoid a speeding Buick. He anticipated Doloris' reaction to Vic's staying out late and leaving her home alone now that their youngest, Angela, had a boyfriend and was out most Friday nights until one or two.

Must be something to have kids, Humbert thought as he went inside and through the skinny hallway between the shoemaker's and

222

the cleaner's, which led to his rooms above Lou's shop. As he climbed the stairs he recalled the pattern of conversation that evening—politics, work, unions, religion, drinking, women, Europe, Paul Palowski who no one had seen for four or five years, sports, weather, and then he remembered how everyone got quiet when he said that about the cold. He liked the way he could tie talk up, neat and tight. He went into his rooms and without turning on any lights walked through the living room and into the kitchen where he set the chair at the table. Then he went into the bedroom, undressed, and lay on top of the bed in his boxer shorts, thinking about Margaret. A faint breeze pushing through the screens in the living room windows, billowing the drapes, flowed through the open door of his bedroom, cooling Oogae's heavy, hairy body. He thought that he might want to marry Maggie, and then he fixed on how she pretended to be offended when he called her that. Humbert "Oogae" Biitner, fifty-six, was snoring loudly ten minutes after he lay down, still uncertain, unresolved, even in his dreams, if he could ask his girlfriend of the past fourteen years if she would marry him.

Margaret Kelleher woke early on Saturday. She did not have to go to the bakery because this and Sunday were her days off. The years of rising near six habited her flesh so that when the dawning sun peeped through the slats of her venetian blinds and the light warmed on and tickled through the long sleeves of her cotton nightgown, she awoke. For Margaret Kelleher, waking was a thing. She stretched her arms back and touched the headboard, then wiggled down farther into the bed until her toes were forced to point out like a ballerina's under the taut sheet and bedspread. Just before she opened her eyes, her full breasts pushed against the sheet and she sighed. That was the only hint, the only intimation of her yearning that she let have sway in her body, that little puff of breath, that slight rise and fall of her breasts. Then she got up.

Margaret slipped into her slippers and yanked the blinds up, letting in the March light still slowed by winter's drag, not bold. She sat at her large, dark vanity and began combing her hair, which hung long and black, the luster unusual for a woman fifty-four. She looked in the mirror as she combed out the tangled strands against her shoulders. Margaret's face was clean white, her skin pure and smooth, wrinkled just around her eyes and mouth, tender lines circling her neck. Her blues eyes set deep behind full, high cheeks. As she noticed, again, her tiny chin that balanced and sharpened the roundness of her face, she said, "That dumb Humbert," and giggled with the thought of her boyfriend's stammering whenever they were alone at night and he tried to be romantic. "Tch, silly baby," she said and got up from the vanity.

After she bathed and dressed, Margaret got busy. She had things to do before Humbert got there for dinner at seven. She mopped and dusted, ran the vacuum cleaner, stopped for something to eat, washed the windows, took the chicken out of the freezer, cleaned some more, and then took another bath. She did everything, even the cooking once she started, with the same intensity, too quick, too precise, bustling around the big, empty house that was her parents' before they died, her father first, then her mother. Cooking at the stove brought Margaret memories of her mother preparing big pots of stew and soup for her husband and her children; eight children—five boys all with light hair like their father; three girls all with black hair like their mother. As she added one slice of butter to the carrots warming on the stove, she muttered about the things that had prevented Oogae from asking her to get married: "First it was his mother, so sick; then my baby brothers; then he lost his job at the post office, tch, wonder how the chicken's doing." She opened the door of the stove and poked the simmering chicken with a long fork, twisting it so that some meat, between the wing and the breast, was dug up and she could see that it was almost ready.

"Son of a bitch if it ain't gonna be late," Humbert Biitner said loud enough so that the three little girls waiting for the bus turned at him with raised eyebrows and opened mouths. He was about to excuse himself when he eyed the bus a couple of blocks away. Then he thought how good it was to live uptown because the bus service to Oakland and downtown was so good, and how he didn't really mind not having a car anymore because it was one less headache, but he knew that a car would make it good for Margaret. He felt a tapping on his side, then a tug on his sweater.

"'Scuse me, Mister. This bus takes us to the library where the muzim'zat?" one of the little girls, about eleven with her hair in long, dark braids, asked Humbert.

"Oh, so you're going to Carnegie Library, are you? This bus'll take you there lickety-split." Oogae made the girls giggle with his ceremonial bow and extended arm, hand open, ushering them onto the bus that had just arrived and sprung open its doors.

During the ride through Soho to Oakland, as the buildings whizzed by, left behind by the passing bus, Humbert thought about Maggie. He was hardly aware of the three girls giggling;

he had no idea they were tittering at him, a slow man, looking older than he was, with a wrinkled, old, brown paper bag under his arm. As he glanced out of the window his mind began to wander. He noticed the age of the houses and buildings, the cracked pavements, and the weeds sprouting dull green along the colorless curbs. Then he saw the river, the brown Monongahela, feeling the wiggle of the water, the shimmer, more than seeing it. Swimming in that river was everything when they were boys, he thought, and the sight of hot smoke, red at night, gray at day, puffing from the mills on the South Side did not threaten their glistening, cold, splashing bodies. He glimpsed the hump of concrete passing in the framed glass and quickly turned his head to look over his shoulder. He saw the bulging Birmingham Bridge spanning the river. He remembered watching the crews in the early '70s dismantle the old iron bridge and he remembered remembering when as little boys they played on, walked across, and dangled from the girders.

Leaving Soho, the bus made the big bend on Forbes and entered Oakland. Humbert looked at the little girls. He watched one brush her cheek on her shoulder, another bury her hands in her lap, and all three of them lean into each other when they shook from laughter. When the bus passed Magee-Womens Hospital and neared the corner of Meyran Avenue, ten minutes after they got on, Humbert did not move to get off. He saw the nervousness of the little girls and knew that for them a bus ride with its getting on and off, was a thing. He wanted to escort them to the library. When they got off the bus he walked them toward the entrance and they giggled some more at his acting so protective. They ran ahead of him, looking back as they approached the library steps. Oogae tipped the thin brim of his hat and winked at the three little girls standing in the entrance. When Humbert turned around to head back toward Margaret's, he felt good.

He walked along Forbes Avenue quickly, past the University of Pittsburgh's huge Cathedral of Learning, anxious to get to Margaret's house for dinner; he suspected that he might be late. As he passed storefronts in the business district, he looked to his left at the reflections of himself mirrored in the panes. He saw an old, fat man with a new sweater, paper bag, and a little green hat that looked comical on his big head. He saw himself pass from pane to pane and behind him, going in the other direction, he also saw reflected the automobiles that were traveling up Forbes Avenue. He felt, without clear reasoning, that he had been like this in his life, moving in different directions, passing things by. Humbert turned left. Halfway down the block he crossed Meyran Avenue, passed between two parked cars, and ran

up the steps to Margaret's house. He knocked
on the door.

Inside, Margaret was wiping the dishes and
utensils at their settings on the table, again.
When she heard the knock she hurried to answer. She stopped in front of the mirror on her
way to the door, admiring her new dress,
brushed a hair off, touched the corners of her
mouth and the ends of her eyebrows with her
fingers. She sighed an impatient breath, partly
out of concern for her meaty belly which hin-
dered the curves of her full hips and breasts.

"Good evening, Maggie," Humbert said
when she opened the door smiling.

"Hello, Humbert." Her eyes shone clear and
sure and in that moment, before he knew that
he would propose tonight, she wondered who
she'd have to invite and the preparations ex-

cited her into a larger smile. She took the paper bag from him and placed it on the big couch in the living room. "You brought your pajamas."

"Can't forget them."

Margaret watched Humbert look around the big room. He glanced at the two upholstered chairs that matched the brown couch of no particular style. He looked at the three gold lamps and their rippled white shades sitting on the end tables. Humbert looked long at the mantle and shelves lined with knickknacks and small porcelain and glass figures of animals, usually arranged in groups of two adults and three or four young—dogs, cats, bears, deer. Little families, he thought. On the high ceiling, Humbert noticed the thin crack that he patched last summer beginning to reopen. He felt an urge to fix the house, to mix a good batch of plaster. Margaret thought about the two empty rooms upstairs, knowing Humbert could fix that, too. She led him toward the dining room. He looked over his shoulders at the tight yellow design of the curtains and noticed how smoothly the color and texture blended with the orange tones of the rug, giving the living room a warm appearance and feel, far different from his bare rooms.

"Cleanin' up today?" He muttered as he realized how obvious his silent inspection must have been.

"I hope you're hungry, Humbert. I made some stuffed chicken." She slid her hand onto his arm; her wrist and the back of her hand nestled against his chest.

"You treat me too well, Maggie." Humbert stopped her before they entered the dining room, leaned down and kissed her on the cheek. She pinched his ribs and he heard her suppressed giggle as they entered the dining room. She knew she had him, knew he was ready. Before he sat at the table, he decided that he would start looking for a used car on

Monday. She has a house, I'll get a car, he thought.

When she came in from the kitchen with the butter and a cold beer for him, Iron City because that was his favorite, Humbert was ready. Intoning that voice of his that was confident and settling, he said to Margaret sitting across the table from him, "Maggie, will you marry me?"

"Pass the carrots, Oogae." Margaret kept her eyes from his, not wanting him to discern her intention of teasing these hours into a wait.

"Huh? Here." He handed the bowl across the table. She spooned seven slices of carrot slowly, though she wanted more. Oogae stared at her sitting. After he had worked up the courage to ask her what he couldn't for fourteen years, he could not understand the precision of her thin, white fingers directing the spoon under three small, orange circles, then four, and the careful placement of the carrots alongside the potato, skin scrubbed pale.

They chewed their food.

"How's the chicken, Humbert?"

"Good. Real good." He swallowed a forkful of breast.

"Good."

"The stuffing's real good, too."

"I made it like you like it. Taste the mushrooms?"

"They're good. Thanks." His voice sailed off.

Margaret chewed some more and seldom raised her eyes from her plate, despite Humbert's glances, impatient grunts, and clinking utensils.

"You better eat, Humbert; your carrots'll get cold. You know how they lose their taste when they're cold."

"I'm gonna buy a car, Mon —"

"Would you like some salad, Humbert?"

"Yeah. Monday."

"Excuse me."

"Yes I would like some salad."

Margaret pushed some salad into the wooden bowl near his plate. "I fixed the dressing that Italian way. I know you like it."

"Thank you."

Oogae finished his meal, his salad, and waited for Margaret. He watched her fork the leaves of lettuce; watched her slice the whole radish until it looked like a tulip with four petals winging around the bulb; watched her soak the wedges of tomato in the bottom of her bowl where the dressing collected; watched her steady fork raise each bit of food to her mouth; and watched her eat. Though he could barely see her chew, inside, behind the drawn cheeks, the pursed lips, that feminine expression, he knew her teeth crunched. Asking her meant admitting he had been afraid to ask her fourteen years ago, last decade; and now, all she did was eat. Humbert Biitner was angry.

"My sister-in-law had a baby. She's going to name her after me because she has black hair. A time of it she had, too. Eighteen hours in labor over at St. Margaret's. You know, at the bottom of that big hill. You know, Michael's wife."

"I proposed and I'm gonna buy a car, Margaret, dammit!"

"Tch! You don't have to swear, Humbert." Margaret feigned offense at Oogae's declaration, continuing her play.

"Well—I'm sorry."

"Well, all right. Would you like dessert now? I made your favorite."

"What? Cheesecake?"

"Yes."

"Thanks."

When Margaret returned from the kitchen with the cake and coffee, Humbert quickly placed the cup in front of him, confident that over coffee and dessert he could ask her again. But she asked.

"Cream?"

"No, Maggie. You don't use sugar, do you, sweet..." his voice cracked "...as you are?"

"Ah." She ate dessert and years later would tell how she didn't remember tasting that cheesecake for watching Oogae squirm.

Oogae was waiting. He waited for a moment of ease, of unconscious silence or natural pause, but it never came. He waited for Margaret to break her rhythmed economy of eating yellow cheesecake and sipping brown coffee, but she did not. When he realized he would not have another chance over supper, after his second cup of coffee, he said, "Well —" and Margaret took advantage of his reticent summary to rise from the table with a perky jump, as if she had been waiting, too.

"I hope you enjoyed everything, Humbert?"

"I did. I did."

"Good. Now you go in there and watch TV. There's a special on channel two; they do singing and dancing from all the old movies. I'm going to red up in here and do the dishes.

"Can I —"

"Now, get in there. It'll just take me a second. You'd be in the way. Now shoo."

Oogae rose from his chair. Margaret was reaching for plates when he took hold of her near her shoulders and turned her to him. She kept her eyes closed until their faces were a breath apart, then opened them to look into Humbert's but his were shut, so she blinked hers shut as they kissed. Oogae slid his big arms around Margaret's back and brought her closer to him. She twisted against his embrace. She pulled her head away from his firm kiss and shook her head.

"Look...what...get...leave...oh," she said.

Oogae opened his eyes and arms.

"Look at us!" Margaret held her arms out, dripping dishes in her hands, looking from her dress to his pants and then at Oogae. "Just look at you, Humbert Biitner." Oogae's pants were wet with melted butter and chicken juice that had dripped from the tilting plates in Margaret's hands.

"Christ," he said.

"Look at me!" Margaret put the dishes on the table and dabbed the butter and juices smeared on the bright flowers of her new blue dress with a napkin.

"What channel you say that dancin's on?" Humbert walked into the living room.

"Two, and change your pants. Don't get my furniture all greasy."

Oogae plucked on the television. He could hear Margaret in the kitchen. He stood in the middle of the living room and sighed, his mind muddled. He had asked her after not having been able for fourteen years, and here he was, alone, in the living room. He put his hands into his pockets and then remembered the grease and stains. He moved toward his bag on the couch because changing his pants was all he could do. He looked through the archway to see if Margaret was in the kitchen. Without taking his shoes off he pulled his gray pants down, folded them, grease spot up, and set them on the arm of the couch. He pulled his pajamas over his shoes, snapped and snugged them beneath his belly, and sat in the chair opposite the television. When he finally focused on the show he saw a chorus line of kicking legs behind a man in a tuxedo with arms outstretched, but the volume was so low that he heard no voice or music. Instead, he heard Margaret scraping plates, running water in the sink, opening and closing the refrigerator, and stamping around. *My wife in the kitchen?* he thought. With her bustle in the background, he watched two routines before his eyes began to droop. They opened for a moment when Margaret slammed the buffet drawer on her folded tablecloth, but his lids soon closed. When she came into the living room he was snoring over the squeaks of the television, chin against chest, in his new black sweater and his pajamas with the red diamond in the black diamond design.

She sat on the couch looking at the huge Oogae slumped in the chair, wondering if her playing had been too harsh, wondering if after fourteen years she could say "Yes." She folded her hands in her lap and settled back. She kicked the cocktail table when she crossed her legs. She watched a few minutes of the dancing before she turned the volume up. When she did, Margaret twirled the knob to maximum, hoping to wake Oogae, then turned it down to a strong, nearly loud level. She peeked over her shoulder as she did this and saw Humbert stir, his snoring interrupted momentarily. She sighed and shook her head, sat down and watched the show. Margaret laughed at the jokes, sang along when she knew some of the words, and cleared her throat between numbers. Oogae snored. When the show was over, Margaret shut the television off. She reached between the couch and Oogae's chair for some sheets, a blanket and a pillow. She tucked the sheets into the couch, fluffed the pillow, and spread the blanket. During all this, her moods flashed from anger to impatience or uncertainty, and her eyes flitted about her work and Oogae's face. She stood in the archway between the living room and the hall, holding his pants.

"Humbert Biitner. Mr. Biitner. Biitner!" Margaret's voice gained pitch and pierce.

"What? What? Huh?"

"Excuse me. I hope you don't mind sleeping on the couch. I know it's not very comfortable." Humbert strained to listen to her as he had nearly every Saturday for the past two years, ever since he was laid off down at the post office and had to sell his car, and instead of taking a bus home and then back again on Sunday for church, he slept over, on that couch.

"It'll be fine, Margaret," Oogae said in a soothing voice.

"'It'll be fine, Margaret.' Tch." She pouted, turned off the lights and hurried up the stairs.

Alone in the dark, Oogae found his bag, changed into his pajama shirt, and lay on the couch, under the blanket. The sheets were cold, and from under the door a draft swirled into the living room. Oogae was tired, his mind spent, and although annoyed by the chilling draft, he was drifting to sleep. His snore was falling into its husky rhythm. Then, Margaret stamped down the steps. She stopped in the entrance and whispered harshly into the living room, "Fourteen years, Oogae Biitner!"

"Jesus Christ!" Oogae bolted up from his sleep. When he looked toward the voice all he heard were Margaret's heavy steps up the stairs.

He settled back to sleep, pulling the blanket up near his face to shield his neck from the draft. I'll never understand these women, he thought. Some minutes in the quiet dark relaxed him, and he began to sleep.

The house, each room was still. A silence pervaded that calmed the old house's creaks and hushed the noise outside on the street. The gentle touch of slippered feet on the stairs made no sound. Then, "Oog-gie, honey," swirled into the room with the chill draft. The soft, sweet, and stretched tones opened Oogae's eyes and he could see Margaret, in the dark, passing through the archway with a fringed shawl over her long sleeping gown. She swayed over to the couch and he closed his eyes. He could feel her warm breath in his ear. "Yes," she whispered her answer and sighed her yearn. Oogae didn't move but continued his steady snore.

Margaret studied his face and thought that he looked like a fat baby lying there, sleeping. She moved away from the couch and went into the kitchen and put on the light. When she came back she clutched her white shawl close to her neck. She stood in the middle of the living room for a moment, then looked over her shoulder at Oogae and whispered, "You cold?" His steady snore was the only response she received. As she walked under the archway her rump jiggled through her clinging cotton nightgown, her figure outlined by the faint light falling from the kitchen. Margaret held down her giggle as she hurried softly up the stairs, breathless.

Oogae opened and then closed his right eye, rolled over, imagining the next morning with Maggie in church, and then conjured a dream of another morning in church when his voice would boom the vows. He knew she was conjuring, too.

FIELDS OF GRACE

He had lost his zeal for travel years ago. But here he was soaring high over the gulf waters with his sister's youngest son on some sort of pilgrimage that he had not planned and would not have taken if his nephew had not been so insistent. *I'm too old for this kind of thing*, Fr. Thomas O'Leary thought and tried to recall the last time he had been on a pilgrimage. *How long ago was that?* he wondered. He remembered taking thirty pilgrims from Our Lady of

Lourdes Parish for a week to Paris and then to that grotto near the Gave River where the Blessed Mother had appeared to Bernadette Soubirous in 1858. A dozen—more than a dozen years ago—and I didn't care much for that trip either, he thought, remembering how the people fawned in prayer near the shrine. He put the duty-free catalogue back in the pouch behind the seat in front of him.

The plane rocked in the turbulent air and stirred the younger priest who had been dozing. "We there yet?" Fr. James Warner's dark, droopy eyes opened slowly to the dull dawn sky that lay beyond his small window.

"Not yet, son." Fr. Thomas tapped his nephew's arm to urge him to continue resting. Fr. Thomas stretched his heavy legs and tilted his seat back trying to find a comfortable position. He adjusted the dial above him so that the stream of air cooled his face. It had been a difficult trip already. They had begun yesterday in

250

Pittsburgh, then missed the connecting flight and endured a long layover in the airport before they could board the next plane out of Miami. *Things've started out badly*, he thought and took it as an omen of worse yet to come. He waved the petite, smiling stewardess away as the refreshment cart rattled by them in the narrow aisle.

He glanced at his nephew sleeping in the seat next to him, his rosaries entwined in his limp fingers. *He's not even thirty; what happened to him?* he wondered. *I sponsored him at Confirmation. He was such an open and idealistic young man before he entered the seminary, but now he's become like all these new priests: so serious and pious, too conservative and zealous.* He remembered the days when he had gone camping with James and his father in the Allegheny National Forest: the exhilaration of hiking in the mountains, canoeing and fishing in the Allegheny, their ranging talks around the camp-

251

fire as they smoked their pipes and listened to the moonlit river. He could almost hear his brother-in-law teasing Jimmy about having a pipe or becoming "a priest like your uncle" and how the teenager just nodded his head and smiled, deflecting the taunts by staring intently into the fire or at his line bobbing in the ripples undulating on the river. *Maybe Sam's death took the joy out of him*, he thought. Jimmy would have loved for his father to have seen him ordained. He closed his eyes, recalling that shrill phone call from his sister, Anne, after she had found out that Samuel had been in that barracks when the scud missile hit and devastated his Greensburg reserve unit. As he dozed off to sleep, he wondered why and how, with so few American deaths in the Persian Gulf War, that stray missile had found his nephew's father.

"This is it!" Fr. James nudged his uncle with his elbow. "Over those fields and on the other side of the mountains and we'll be in the city. Take a look, Unc."

Fr. Thomas woke up slightly disoriented. He could feel the pressure building in his ears as they descended. He leaned across his nephew's seat to peer out the little window to the great expanse of colorless earth that lay beneath them. The morning sky was heavy and bleak over the gray October fields that stretched monotonously to the foot of the mountains. "Kind of flat," he heard himself mumble. *Not at all what I expected*, he thought. He had never been to Mexico.

Fr. Thomas was tired after the long flight. As they departed the plane and he breathed the hot, heavy air, he felt stifled by the hundreds of small, dark bodies pressing in all around him at the terminal. His nephew handled the Spanish deftly at the baggage claim and the passport counter, but it still took over an hour to get out of the airport. "So, this is where all the

Volkswagen beetles are," he said as their cab pushed through Mexico City in the congested morning traffic, horns resounding across the hazy boulevards, thousands of people criss-crossing every which way. After an ambling drive through the teeming city, their driver finally found the *Casa Sacerdotal de la Basilica de Santa Maria de Guadalupe*, a couple blocks from the shrine down a side street. Fr. James paid the fare and tipped their driver generously. Fr. Thomas' legs ached as they followed the porter up the stairs to their clean, gracious suite. Despite his nephew's eagerness to see the nearly five-hundred-year-old *tilma* with the miraculous image of the Blessed Virgin Mary, Fr. Thomas persuaded him to unpack and freshen up. The older man was perspiring and wanted nothing more than to wash the grime from his body and take a *siesta*.

Following the midday meal, it was late in the afternoon sun before they finally walked out onto the steamy streets of Mexico City in their clerics, the younger priest a stride ahead of his uncle.

"I can't wait to see it," Fr. James said. "It's like an icon painted by the hand of God."

"Uh-hunh." Fr. Thomas was distracted by a pair of scrawny, emaciated dogs sleeping in front of a garage as they turned the corner. The sun beat down mercilessly on the animals, bright and hot.

As they approached the grounds of the Basilica, they could see the people milling about the plaza around the church. A slight woman in a black shawl and her three children with eyes like deer sat at the entrance of the plaza begging for alms.

"This is it—I can't believe we're here," the young man said and quickened his pace. "Look at all these people."

Fr. Thomas pulled at his starched collar to ease the itch of perspiration around his neck.

They're smaller than I imagined, Fr. Thomas thought as they passed a group of local pilgrims boarding a bus.

"*Buenos dias*," the younger priest said with a slight bow of his head in response to their shy glances.

"Jim, they're staring because they're not used to seeing priests in clerics on the street—let alone Americans," Fr. Thomas said to his nephew. "Ever since the revolution began before the First World War the Church in Mexico has been suppressed. Even this pilgrimage site is run by the government..."

"C'mon, Unc, let's go," the younger man urged as they approached the doors to the Basilica.

"I'm coming," he said aloud, then muttered. "*Gringo*."

Inside the huge Basilica they had to squint their eyes to adjust from the brilliant sunlight to the cool shadows of the church. The younger man dipped his fingers into the holy water fount and blessed himself with the sign of the cross. As they stood within the large modern building surveying the space, Fr. Thomas could not get over the appearance of the hundreds of Mexicans in the confessional lines, kneeling in prayer, laying flowers at side altars, shuffling reverently all around them: copper-colored skin, high cheekbones, black, straw-like hair. His nephew was head and shoulders taller than the biggest of them. He heard the murmur of Spanish prayers faintly echoing within the Basilica.

"It's up there." Fr. James pointed to the far wall beneath the vaulted ceiling. "Above and behind the sanctuary."

As they moved past a tour group in the middle of the round church, Fr. James' voice softened to a hush. "I can't believe it—there it is," he whispered in wonder.

They're more Indian than Spanish, Fr. Thomas thought, continuing his observation of the Mexican pilgrims.

When they stopped at the edge of the large sanctuary, they could see the framed cloak high above the altar, but the face and features were not clear from that distance.

"We can go around the side behind the sanctuary for a closer look," Fr. James directed his uncle. "They have some sort of viewing area—I read about it in the tour book."

Fr. Thomas was intrigued by the posture and attitude of the Virgin of Guadalupe emblazoned on the sacred cloth. "Just a minute," he said to his nephew distractedly, drawn by her image. He held his breath for a while, then sighed in exhalation. He stood quiet and still for a moment.

When they got to the corridor behind the sanctuary, several pilgrims were gliding on the half-dozen people movers that passed before and beneath the revered peasant *tilma* of Blessed Juan Diego.

"Oh, my God," Fr. James muttered, his dark, intense eyes wide with amazement.

Fr. Thomas stood to the side of the rails, staring intently at the life-sized image of the Mother of God. His heart raced. His nephew was already gliding beneath the *tilma* on the people movers, once, twice, then again. Though he was self-conscious of being trans-fixed by the image, Fr. Thomas could not take his blue eyes from the *tilma*, holding the image like a memory: her *mestizo* face so benign, al-most sad in its beauty; her delicate hands folded in prayer; her blue, starry mantle draped about her bowed head and gentle figure with grace; her printed gown modest and muted, yet colorful; her black hair peeking out from her veiled head; and the light—the light all around her.

Fr. Thomas followed his nephew onto the people mover, gazing upward as they glided by the beautiful image emanating from the rough cloth. When they got off, the older priest bumped into a small, pregnant woman with a child trying to ease by him.

"Excuse me," he said and touched her shoulder, embarrassed by his paunch.

"*Padre*," she said and drew her dark shawl about her as she guided her child past him.

"There's a eucharistic chapel around the side, here," Fr. James said and took his uncle by the elbow. "Let's pray together for a while."

As they ascended the ramp leading out of the corridor, Fr. Thomas O'Leary took a long, last look at the miraculous image of the Blessed Mother emblazoned on the coarse peasant fabric ornately framed in bronze, silver, and gold. *She's beautiful*, he thought.

In the chapel, he slouched in the pew, while his nephew pulled out his rosary and knelt in adoration before the tabernacle housing the Lord. Fr. Thomas was weak and a little dizzy, his eyes aching, unable to offer articulate prayer. He was vaguely aware of the people around them scattered in the other pews: young men, women with children. He closed his eyes. A deep, resonant tone seemed to sound within him. He could see the haunting image of the Blessed Virgin Mary in his mind's eye.

A few minutes passed and when he opened his eyes he felt like he was returning from somewhere. He smelled the fragrance of the fresh roses in vases near the tabernacle amid the hundreds of burning candles. Everything looked different, more distinct, except his nephew seated in the chapel pew next to him. Even the quality of light seemed altered, more soft and diffused. He looked toward the tabernacle. "My Lord and my God," he whispered in prayer. He noticed the large, powerful fresco of the Holy Trinity for the first time: the vigorous Christ triumphant with burial wrappings unfurling about him, poised at his Father's strong hand, a dove-like fire blazing between them.

"You ready?" the younger priest asked his uncle.

"Let's go," he nodded. "I'm hungry."

Outside, they stood beyond the large Basilica doors looking out across the evening plaza partially filled with pilgrims, the sun still hot and relentless.

"Look at them." Fr. James motioned with his head. "They walk on their knees across the cobblestone plaza in reparation for their sins or to invoke the Virgin's intercession on the day their children are baptized. It's twice as long as a football field."

Fr. Thomas peered out over the host of pilgrims. The people moving from side to side as they moved toward the Basilica on their knees, others ambling about them in the plaza, looked like a great field of grain swaying to and fro in the merciful evening breeze. Fr. Thomas was touched by the devotion of these Mexican pilgrims despite his usual cynicism.

As they walked back to the *Casa Sacerdotal*, the priests bought some bottled water from a vendor, gulping it down as they quietly made their way up the street. They walked by a young couple holding hands on a bench, the mother placing bits of food in the mouths of their two small children.

After the simple evening meal, shared with only a few of the dozen priests who lived at the *Casa* and served the Basilica, Fathers Thomas and James retired to their rooms.

"I liked that Raphael," the younger one said as they climbed the stairs, referring to the Columbian friar who spoke with them over beans and rice. "He was friendly and talkative."

"Ah, you'd like anybody named after an angel," Fr. Thomas said. He enjoyed teasing his nephew about his piety, among other things. "You liked that pretty cook, too. I heard you charming her with your Spanish."

Fr. James blushed. "Asking for another cup of coffee is hardly flirting," Fr. James countered once they were inside their suite. He picked up his copy of St. John of the Cross' *Dark Night of the Soul*. "I'm going to read a little."

"I'm going to bed," Fr. Thomas said with a tinge of pride for his nephew's youthful adventurousness that had gotten them to Mexico. "I'm beat. Good night, Jim."

"Mass in the little chapel downstairs before we leave for the shrine, tomorrow," Fr. James said. "Good night, Unc."

Fr. Thomas washed and changed quickly. He smoked a pipe to help him unwind from the day. His senses were buzzing with stimuli from the afternoon's tour of the shrine. He fell asleep shortly after he slipped between the sheets, mumbling the "Hail Mary," the droning of the city's endless traffic rising to him through the open windows of the night.

And as he drifted off to sleep, he glided across autumn fields, swaying at the river's edge, entranced by the undulation of the water, moonlight spangling on the ripples; and he was waiting for something, anticipating the emergence, when the water broke in a fury and the huge hands clasping the golden chalice breached the river, the water spilling over the lip turning blood red as it cascaded in streams from the cup, the splash changing the waters to a river of light glistening up and down stream. "Kit-tan-ne," she breathed. And Fr. Thomas awoke in a sweat in the dark night, reaching out across that mysterious, gleaming river of light that haunted his dreams, the woman's enchanting voice echoing in his ears: "Kit-tan-ne."

The next day, after they concelebrated morning Mass and had a breakfast of sweet rolls and coffee, they got an early start as Fr. James was determined to get a thorough look at all the buildings and grounds of the Basilica shrine. Along the way, they passed the two ugly dogs sleeping in front of the garage. As they strode across the cobblestone plaza, Fr. Thomas recalled his luminous dream from the night before. "Kit-tan-ne," he whispered more than once, enjoying the mysterious evocation of the word from some foreign tongue or other. *What does it mean?* he thought. The original basilica was in disrepair, scaffolding and ropes surrounding the sinking foundation. So they ventured into the small Indian chapel, a stone's throw away, where tens of thousands of Indian converts had been baptized since the sixteenth century. Something about the small chapel of the Indians intrigued Fr. Thomas. Children played about the stone monument.

Fr. James translated the plaques and markers for his uncle, unfolding the story of Bishop Zumarraga, the *tilma* full of roses, the miraculous events of 1531, and the millions of converts who entered the Church in the decade following the apparitions. The younger priest led them through the beautifully manicured gardens to the outdoor display dramatizing the Virgin Mary's appearance to Blessed Juan Diego on the side of Tepeyac Hill. The figures were larger than life-size; the government kept this tourist site immaculate, almost too neat and clean.

They stopped for something to drink at the refreshment stand and sat under an umbrella shading their table from the blazing heat. Fr. Thomas wondered if the woman's voice in his dream was supposed to be the voice of Our Lady of Guadalupe. He thought he heard her breathe that word again, "Kit-tan-ne," like a whisper or locution. Resting awhile, the two priests discussed their impressions and their plans for the rest of the day. But while they tried to talk around it for a while, eventually their polarity surfaced; it always did: liberal/conservative, pastoral/dogmatic, skeptical/loyal. That dichotomous tension revealed itself in most everything they said. Fr. Thomas was growing irritated with his nephew's penchant for order, for giving directions, and for insisting that they explore all the grounds before it got too hot. *Why is he so hellbent on accomplishing systematically what would happen anyhow if we just took things more casually?* he thought. Nonetheless, he agreed to climb to the top of Tepayac Hill to see the other chapel, in exchange for a walk through the open-air market adjacent to the grounds of the shrine. They meandered through the hundreds of little makeshift vending booths that sold leather goods, roasting meats and rice, hammered metal trinkets, bottled water and sodas, earthen vessels, and images of the Virgin of Guadalupe on everything from tee-shirts to bumper stickers, from painted glass to key chains. Fr. Thomas bought a hand-worked leather belt and a keychain before Fr. James prevailed upon him to complete their course.

The path was steep and ambling along the hillside. Fr. Thomas could feel the grade in his legs and the heat rising from the walkway. Slowly, they ascended the hill alongside the other pilgrims, following the circuitous path that went first one way and then the other. They stopped a couple of times for Fr. Thomas to catch his breath, which only further irritated the older priest, reminding him that he was approaching sixty. The sunlight was intense through his white, thinning hair and on his fair skin. When at last they reached the hilltop, they panned the vast view of the sprawling city lying beneath the canopy of haze and smog that hung perennially over the millions of people. The largest city in the world stretched before their eyes to the mountains on the horizon. They stood beneath the four colossal archangels chiseled from blocks of stone and perched on the hilltop like sentinels. The huge hands and arms of the statues conjured Fr. Thomas's dream of the breaching chalice in the river of light. *What did it mean?* he thought as they toured the little chapel with its hundreds of painted angels beautifully decorating the ceiling, the walls and the columns. "Kit-tan-ne," he heard the whisper again. Crutches, photographs, and handmade cards were laid randomly at the feet of angelic statues, marking petitions and gratitude, testimonies to inexplicable healings. Fr. James was deeply moved by these personal displays of devotion, while Fr. Thomas regarded them as naïve piety at best or superstition at worst. They stopped to pray awhile before they started their descent. Halfway down the hill, they took another path that passed beneath a line of trees, shading them from the harsh noonday sun. A few beggars, resting against the trunks, reached their hands out in supplication. Fr. Thomas gave them some coins. Tired and hot, a little irritable, at last the two priests found themselves nearing the Basilica, in front of an enormous metal statue of Pope John Paul II, nearly as large as the archangels on Tepayac Hill. They stood in the shadow cast by the statue. Fr. Thomas wiped his face with a handkerchief.

"He's great," Fr. James said, marveling at the huge statue of John Paul II in full papal regalia. "I mean he's probably going to be considered the greatest pope of the twentieth century—one of the most important in the history of the Church."

Fr. Thomas turned away from his nephew's excited chatter, trying to avoid that lightning rod for the tensions that had been crackling between them the past couple of days, the past couple of years.

"It says here that this was erected following his visit to Mexico City back in the first year of his pontificate," Fr. James translated for his disinterested uncle. "When it's all over, I'll betcha Church historians will be calling him Pope John Paul the Great; I just know it."

"Get off of it, Jimmy," Fr. Thomas protested, irritated with his nephew's hasty judgment. "He's too rigid, too narrow, too Polish. He's no Paul VI, that's for sure."

"Too narrow? Where have you been for the last twenty years?" the younger man insisted. His hand gestured toward the statue. "He's leading the Church into a new millennium. He's restored the fullness of Catholicism—the fullness that your generation tried to destroy after the Council."

Fr. Thomas was stung by the ferocity of his nephew's rebuttal, the intensity out of proportion to the topic. Yet, he could not refrain from defending his generation of the Church against Fr. James' denunciation. "Where have *I* been? Where have *I* been? Trying to bring the gospel to the market place; trying to make it meaningful for people; trying to make it—relevant," he hesitated over the word.

"Oh, right, 'relevant'." Fr. James raised his hands in mock adulation. "All you made it was mundane and banal. That's why half the people don't go to church anymore. Your generation relativized the truth; you sacrificed the sacred mysteries on the altar of relevancy."

A small crowd of Mexicans stopped to watch and hear the American priests gesticulating wildly and arguing in loud tones, though the English words were lost on them.

"What do you know, anyhow?" Fr. Thomas said, getting personal. "How long have you been a priest? Three, four years? The oils haven't even dried yet."

"Long enough to recognize a fraud when I see one!" Fr. James was trembling, tears welling up in his red, contorted face. He looked at his uncle as if he was going to say something, but then he turned away and strode back up Tepeyac Hill, leaving Fr. Thomas shocked and hurt beneath the shadow of the Pope's statue.

Fr. Thomas watched his nephew roughly push by some slow-moving people, watched him grow smaller as he ascended the path, eventually disappearing among the throng of pilgrims. His nephew's inappropriate outburst upset him deeply. He was hurt and embarrassed. He shuffled into the Basilica more to get away from the site of their conflict than to go into the church. He found himself walking toward the eucharistic chapel with the fresco of the Holy Trinity. He knelt down and held his head in his shaking hands; a feeling of abandonment, estrangement from the Lord, overwhelmed him. "Where have I been for the last twenty years?" he prayed in desperation out of the apathy that held him like a vice. He knew he had lost his passion for his priestly work, for the Church, for the mystery of the sacraments, for everything save the measurable administrative efficiency that always distinguished his pastorates. He thought of his friends and classmates who had left the priesthood in past years. Their leaving had been painful for him, causing him to question his own vocation. "Where have I been?"

Back at the *Casa*, in his bedroom, Fr. Thomas heard the door to their suite open, signaling his nephew's return. He felt bad that he had permitted the heat of the day and the argument to lead to personal insults. He heard Jim's bedroom door close softly. He loved his nephew like he was his own son. But Jim had touched a nerve, exposing his slow, ambivalent drift from the Church the past twenty years:

his failure to maintain his reading, his disaffection with the Holy Father, his struggle with prayer: his acedia. He knew his nephew was right: his spiritual life felt empty and false; his prayer had grown dry and infrequent. He had promised his sister that he would always look out for him after Sam's death, help him mature as a man and a priest. It would be a challenge now. And he thought he understood what was going on in James, too, his wise, paternal heart moved with compassion for his nephew's railing against the death of his father that had wounded him and left him vulnerable, ranting against the fears of his young life, against the chaos of the world he inherited from a previous generation, his generation. Fr. Thomas thought he could hear a trace of that railing in his nephew's every dogmatic declaration, every pious pronouncement—even when he was right. He knew that he would have to be the first to make a move toward reconciliation, to reach across that generational divide. He thought of Samuel and how much he had been like the brother he never had. He recalled their camping trips in the forest, fishing on the river with little Jimmy, and he remembered something about the nights around the campfire, the ritual of Sam and him lighting up their pipes while the boy looked on in awe, wanting to be a man like his father, like his uncle. He smiled with the memory of the boy's urgency. We'll have a pipe, he thought and gathered up his tobacco.

Fr. Thomas rapped three times on Fr. James' door. The young priest came to the door in his tee-shirt and shorts, his dark eyes droopy with sleep.

"C'mon, Jim," Fr. Thomas said. "I got a surprise for you. Put on your robe."

"Hunh?" Fr. James said.

The older priest led the younger man up the stairway a couple of flights, then out onto a small patio that opened onto the dusk. He pointed to a short ladder that rose to the roof of the *Casa*. "You first."

"What are we doing?" Fr. James said as he climbed up the first few rungs in his slippers.

"Never mind," the older priest said. "Just go." He followed his nephew up the ladder to the flat rooftop.

"Wow!" James said. "This is magnificent."

Before them, in the half-light of dusk, Mexico City sprawled and gleamed as faint lights glimmered here and there among the myriad of buildings that stretched indistinctly to the horizon.

"Twenty-five million people," Fr. James said. "She sure knew what she was doing."

"Here." Fr. Thomas handed one of the packed pipes to his nephew.

"I don't smoke," he said.

"It's about time," Fr. Thomas said and struck a match. "Just draw on this a few times."

"All right, Unc," the younger priest said. He drew on the pipe several times as his uncle held the match above the bowl of tobacco. The young man coughed.

"Don't inhale," Fr. Thomas laughed. "You'll kill yourself."

The smoke curled heavenward like incense as they puffed on their pipes, looking out onto the wondrous expanse of the city glittering under the patina created by the dusk light diffused through the cloud of smog that hung over that intricate, urban matrix nestled in the prairie basin.

"I'm sorry, Uncle Thomas," Fr. James said. "Sorry for the awful things I said to you this afternoon."

"I'm sorry, too, Jim," Fr. Thomas said. "Sorry for fighting with you."

"Sometimes, I get too full of myself," the young man said.

"Sometimes, I'm not full enough," the old priest said.

Then they talked about how seminary life had changed so much in a generation, and they exchanged stories of their priestly lives, stories of babies wailing during homilies, couples fighting at wedding rehearsals, anointings in the emergency room, ushers forgetting the second collection, the hard funeral of a young mother or father. With the darkening of the evening, the glow of dusk hovered around them on the rooftop and gave the city a golden sheen. Like some old chief and his brave warrior, they smoked their pipes, making peace with each other, with the passage of time, with the Church, with God, until their talk came around to where it was supposed to go in the first place.

"I miss my Dad," Fr. James said. "I miss him a lot."

"I know," Fr. Thomas said. "I miss him, too."

Something passed between them as they smoked their pipes, something ancient yet alive. They had found a place of their own, a sympathy beyond the world yet surely in it, a grace that bound them to each other, forever. They were priests according to the order of Melchizedek, a bond even deeper than the common blood that coursed through their veins. They took their last puff and then prayed together on the rooftop looking out over that seemingly endless field of gold that glimmered and sparkled to the night's horizon.

That night, Fr. Thomas slept soundly, resting his body and mind, his heart and soul, in the grateful peace they had made. On the flight home the next afternoon, Fr. Thomas kept recalling those ten thousand morning worshippers gathered in the new *Basilica de Santa Maria de Guadalupe* as he and James concelebrated the special thirtieth anniversary Mass of its solemn dedication. He remembered the orderless throng of veiled and black-haired Mexicans flocking to him to receive communion, babes in arms, their upturned faces full of faith in the midst of their want. And when he had distributed communion, he had felt the power of the Body and Blood of Christ to keep each of them afloat in that vast sea of drowning humanity, beleaguered but not beaten, on their pilgrimage to heaven. Throughout the flight, he glanced over toward James, who sat brooding over his breviary, and whose dark features and hair reminded him so much of Samuel. As they flew together across the Gulf waters, he knew that something had happened to him in Mexico, something that he did not quite understand, something deeply spiritual and enduring. Soaring high above the earth, he had an intimation that somehow the ground had shifted beneath him.

Back home at Our Lady of Lourdes in Pittsburgh, the letter had been on his desk for a couple of days before he was there to open it. Father Babinez had died suddenly, there were financial problems at the parish, and the bishop wanted him to become the new pastor in Kittanning. Without hesitation, he called the bishop's office to confirm the appointment; he intuited that it was the right time to go. Then he had called his nephew with the news of the transfer that he knew the young man would interpret as a great portent from God. The two had talked excitedly about the name of the parish, the fresh prospects, the river. And in that exchange with his nephew a newfound joy began to rise in his heart.

Fr. Thomas clutched the letter in his hand as he drove in the dusk along the Allegheny River Valley ablaze with autumn colors. This was the

only church in Western Pennsylvania named
after Our Lady of Guadalupe and the coinci-
dence did not escape him. He had seen the colorful mosaic before in the eucharistic chapel,
detailing the whole story of the apparitions,
the *tilma*, and the massive conversions in the
decade that followed.

"Kit-tan-ne," he repeated like the woman in
the dream. "Kit-tan-ning," he said deliberately,
recognizing the anglicized version of the Indian
name for the original Delaware village along
the Allegheny—before the French or English
ever settled there. His new keychain with the
image of the Virgin of Guadalupe dangled from
the steering column as he continued up Route
28. When he got to the town he parked the car
a couple blocks from the church on Water
Street. He walked along the concrete path con-
structed near the water's edge in the new
Riverfront Park, pulling his jacket collar up

high on his neck as the cool, October night descended.

Folding his hands, he looked out into the blackness, peering toward the hidden fields of grace that lay beyond the moonlit river like a promise:

> *On a dark night*
> *kindled in love, with yearning,*
> *I set out, oh happy chance.*
> *My house being now at rest.*

He recited the first few lines of a poem from St. John of the Cross that he had forgotten he ever knew. A fish splashed on the shimmering river, beckoning. *A little farther north; a little older*, he thought. *Same river.* And he knew that he would raise the cup of mercy, he would, again, labor in the fields for that harvest of souls that awaited him, awaited a priest of God.

TRUE COLORS

They had been gone awhile; he was the last one left save for the unkempt vagrant mumbling something in the nave. The late afternoon sun cast a soft red light through the stained-glass windows that illumined the colorful murals and floor tiles. He walked along the balcony railing, noting the flickering play of the May light glittering along the gilded edges of the ceiling, arches, and pillars. St. Joseph Cathedral held strong memories of his priesthood, but that dark emptiness was with him, again, in this sacred place where he used to be lifted to God.

Earlier that spring afternoon, Fr. Daniel Morton brought a few adults down from his parish in Follansbee to Wheeling for the Sacrament of Confirmation with Bishop William Clement, the same kind and holy man who had ordained him in the Cathedral a dozen years ago, before it had been so beautifully restored. *Do you promise obedience to me and my successors?* he recalled the old man asking in such a gentle way that his limpid blue eyes drew the promise from him even more than his words asked the question. "Yes," he whispered, again, the vow sounding a little hollow in the empty Cathedral.

As he descended the circular staircase, Fr. Daniel felt remorse for letting down the good Bishop. He wondered if that holy man sensed his ambivalence: something about the force of his crimson embrace at the sign of peace during Mass made him feel guilty—an unspoken spiritual empathy passing between them in the midst of the sacred mysteries. He picked up his alb from the coat rack in the narthex where he had hung it before going upstairs, not wanting to get the white garment soiled negotiating the narrow, winding passage. He flung it over his arm, blessing himself with the holy water, and pushed open the large door to the bright spring day.

The day's light was obscured by the dark figure lurking at his feet. He saw him sitting there on the steps of the Cathedral: dirty and idle, foul and waiting. The hairs on the back of Fr. Daniel's neck stood up. How did he get here so fast, he thought, his confusion as strong as his instinctive revulsion. He leaned away from the crouching man and tried to step by him, but as soon as the wastrel opened his mouth, the young priest knew that he would have to reckon with this one.

"You're closer to Satan than me," the vile words came up out of the rumple of garments and bags that covered him, his voice too certain for his condition. Though he turned his aspect slightly toward Fr. Daniel, the priest did not get a clear look at the man's bearded face as his abrupt accusation stung his conscience. "You won't give God what He wants."

The Cathedral door closed shut behind the priest. He leaned his tall body against it, his breaths coming quickly. He clutched his alb to his chest as if it were a shield. A lone car ambled by the Cathedral on this Sunday afternoon but everything beyond that odd encounter seemed muted and hazy to him, so real was the vagrant hunched at his feet. As abruptly as he had addressed the priest, the man returned to his tattered bags, balled up in his sloppy overcoat that hid any discernable shape in a colorless lump like some medieval gargoyle protruding from the base of the church. Fr. Daniel felt his heart pounding in his chest as he looked at the man, speechless. He pulled open the large Cathedral door and retreated inside. He strode toward the safety of the sanctuary and knelt at the steps, peering across the altar toward the tabernacle shadowed beneath the marble baldacchino. His mind was a jumble of inarticulate thoughts and phrases as he tried to recall exactly what that horrid man had said to him, tried to understand what it meant. "Closer to Satan…" he muttered "…give God what He wants." He bowed his head. The "Hail Mary" rose to his lips. After a brief time of silent prayer, Fr. Daniel opened his dark eyes to the radiant sanctuary mural of the regal, red-robed Christ amidst his saints and angels, enthroned on his cathedra in glory, the penetrating colors deep and dazzling since the lifting of the soot and smoke. A trace of that putrid smell lingered in his nostrils; he knew that he had to face him.

A calmer Fr. Daniel got up and walked back down the aisle to confront the vagabond. When he opened the Cathedral door a cool spring breeze brushed his cheek, but the man was gone. He looked up and down the street; he walked to the nearest intersection at Thirteenth. The streets were virtually empty. The man was nowhere to be found; he seemed to have vanished into thin air somewhere on the streets of downtown Wheeling.

Through the week, Fr. Daniel was restless and irritable: on Monday, he canceled his appointments and spent most of his day in his suite, brooding; on Tuesday and Thursday his concentration was scattered as he reviewed annulment cases at the Marriage Tribunal in the chancery; on Wednesday, at the parents' meeting for First Communion, he was unprepared and grew angry when one of the mothers asked if her daughter could wear gloves; at morning Mass he was distracted and lost his place a few times; and at the Ultreya luncheon on Friday, he could not bring himself to join in the singing of "De Colores" with the other *cursillistas*. At night, his restless sleep was plagued by that troubling dream of Ryan's helpless hand going down in the swirling river beyond his desperate grasp, lost in the churning current, as he, Beth, and the children drifted to safety in the raft. On Friday afternoon, he snapped at Madeline, his secretary, for a minor typing error on a cover letter to the diocese with the statistical profile of the parish. So, with Fr. Innocent Uju at St. Anthony's to celebrate and preach the weekend masses on mission appeal for the Diocese of Arua, Uganda, Fr. Daniel gave him the keys and asked him to hear noon confessions so that he could drive to the Cheat River where it all began, where, he thought, he would come to a decision.

On Saturday morning, Fr. Daniel put on the wrong color vestments, donning the green of ordinary time rather than the martyr's red. After Mass, he abruptly excused himself from Mrs. Keating's insistent prattle about the Guild's upcoming card party; he was anxious to get on the road. Before he left town, he stopped by the Follansbee Dock Systems plant to have a word with Red, one of his maintenance volunteers, about the leak in the boiler room of the church. Eventually, out of his blacks, he set out across the cobblestoned streets of Follansbee for the ride south through Wheeling, then the longer stretch east to the other side of Morgantown and the river. On the open road, as Fr. Daniel cruised along Route 2 in his forest green LeSabre, he kept conjuring the scene of his terrified friend engulfed in the frothing waters of the Cheat River, almost a year to the day of his death. Driving parallel to the Ohio River through the panhandle of West Virginia, Fr. Daniel passed beneath a coaling tower and glanced across the wide river bordering the states, wondering if the pasture might be greener on the other side. His mind was racing with conflicting thoughts that kept settling on the wrong answer: Beth and the children. Maybe I should leave and marry her, he thought, as he passed through the town of Warwood, where he had served at Corpus Christi Parish when he was first ordained. And though he never said it aloud, hidden in his confused thoughts, just below his consciousness, lurked the impulse that he could fill the void and take Ryan's place. Once on the other side of Wheeling and heading southeast, he turned on the radio to soothe his feverish mind. He heard the finish of a popular new song by some folksinger in the tristate area: "Put your hand to the plow and don't look back," she sang in her sweet, plaintive voice, the song an encouraging ballad for faithfulness to the gospel. *Yeah, I heard you, God,* he thought in self-recrimination. For the next hour, or so, he sped along the smooth, snaking highway trying *not* to think, the dense foliage green and lush on the May mountains. Try as he might, though, he could not help slipping into that analytical habit of mind that seemed to be too much a part of his interior life these days, filling up the place in his heart where he should have been surrendering to God in prayer. *I spend too much time in my head,* he thought. Wavering in his commitment to the priesthood, Fr. Daniel Morton took note of the duplicity that was distancing him from the Lord.

Once on the other side of Morgantown, he drove faster to get to the river valley. The Appalachian countryside became more mountainous, the roads more winding, as he neared the Cheat. A lot of outdoor enthusiasts were also making their way to the weekend water. He drove to the top of Snake Hill Road and then down again to the river. He parked his car at the first spot on the roadside that he could find. He got out and started walking through the thick brush toward Devil's Bend where Ryan had gone down. As he got closer, he could hear the haunting roar of the whitewater and see the peaks of foam through the green thicket. Then he smelled the river. Standing in a small clearing near the riverbank, Fr. Daniel's dark eyes stared intently into the deadly waters splashing against the large rocks protruding from the Cheat, menacingly. He had come to this spot many times over the past year to pray for Ryan's soul and to ask God to ease his guilty conscience, which had accused him ever since the accident occurred. I could've saved him, he thought, failing to pray. His hand slipped through mine. I could've saved him. For the thousandth time, he recalled the circumstances of his friend's death: how Ryan had wanted to go whitewater rafting like they had done so often when they went to Wheeling-Jesuit together and would drive to the Cheat on spring weekends. Ryan was always pushing the limits, trying to recapture some of that recklessness that had invigorated their youth. They had been cautioned by radio reports of the river hazard after the heavy rains, but they decided to risk it anyhow, for old time's sake. In his mind's eye, Fr. Daniel could still see Beth in her blue jeans and white blouse with the kids waving to them in the driveway of the cottage as they pulled out of the gravel lot: the young mother holding her baby girl on her hip, her hand tenderly about her son's shoulders, pressing him to her side, her long, light hair blowing in the spring breeze, a premonition of dread in her forced smile.

He walked along the rugged bank, the river's spray misting his warm face. He saw a family having a picnic at a clearing across the waters, their voices lost in the roar of the roiling river. He remembered Beth's shocked face when he first told her after they found Ryan's limp and twisted body on the bank several hundred yards down stream. He remembered holding the children, but there was no consoling Beth as her shoulders trembled in shocked abjection, the tears coming later. She and Ryan had been sweethearts since their first days at Wheeling-Jesuit University. He recalled his first impression of that suited couple when he met them after one of Fr. Desmond's freshman philosophy classes: a match made in heaven, he thought, their gestures and words, their posture and animation, so complementary: the couple exuding a kind of empathetic harmony like in a graceful dance. His revelry was interrupted when some whitewater rafters came barreling down the river toward Devil's Bend. He watched them negotiate the terrifying turn in the Cheat's course that had claimed his friend's life last year, and others before him. The s-curve in the river was bad enough, but then the low falls spilling onto the jagged rocks made it even more treacherous. He watched until he could see all three bright green rafts of thrill-seekers emerge beyond the rocks to the deeper waters of the Cheat. He let out his breath.

Fr. Daniel found a rock ledge to sit on as he peered into the raging river that had claimed the life of his friend like some ancient pagan deity exacting human sacrifice for passage. The guilt for accepting Ryan's reckless dare and then being unable to pull him out when he went under plagued his conscience, again, as it had innumerable times over the past year. Some tears fell from the corners of his eyes, mingling with the fine river spray misting his face. The bright sun peeked out momentarily from the heavy clouds, the light spangling on the water. Over the past year, he had found himself spending more time with Beth, little Nate, and Samantha, trying to fill the void of Ryan's loss, trying to reassure himself that they did not blame him for his death.

"Daddy Dan," the children took to calling him after a few months, compensating in their naïve yet ingenious way for the loss of their father. Like the pull of some powerful vortex swirling in the Cheat, he had felt himself drawn into their vulnerable lives, unable or unwilling to extricate himself from that familial whirlpool of love and loss, fear and fragility, in which they were drowning. "Why, God? Why? Why Ryan?" he railed more than prayed. I can't leave them alone, he thought. I have to help them. There's no one to take care of them. He was frightened by the realization that he would consider leaving the priesthood to be with Beth, assuming that she would want him. He felt a compulsion to protect Ryan's son and daughter from more of the cruelties of life that threatened them in this fallen world.

An hour passed under the overcast skies, his conflicted heart as tumultuous as the rapids of the Cheat. He saw another group of rafters tempting the river, saw them drifting down the green valley toward Devil's Bend. His body lay tired and motionless on the rocks from the tension of the past months as that war of vows and friendship, guilt and love, raged in his mind. Fr. Daniel realized that his priesthood was mortally wounded and that the Church was losing the battle, as he fell into an exhausted and foreboding doze, the rushing river roaring in his ears. Drifting into a dark sleep, he sensed a seething scowl looming above him, the dreadful weight upon his chest, the inexorable press of sin pinning him to that hopeless rock, until he woke in a sweaty panic flailing his arms and panting, looking about him, only to see the rustling of the breeze through the thicket. Instinctively, he made the sign of the cross.

Then two fishermen clomping through the loam in their hip-boots stopped in the clearing a stone's throw away. "You okay?" one of them called to him.

Fr. Daniel stared past the men, unable to respond, disoriented by what he took to be a vivid and frightening daydream.

The man raised his fishing rod and the two of them continued through the brush.

Dazed, Fr. Daniel sat on the rock ledge for a few minutes, until the roaring Cheat brought him back to his senses. He had the vague feeling that his life was in danger, somehow, that someone wanted to hurt him. He looked over his shoulder as he got up, as if he expected to see something lurking in the brush. He quickly returned to his car.

On the ride back he stopped for something to eat at the Bob Evans Family Restaurant. He took a couple of bites of the fried chicken but left the biscuits untouched on his plate. He asked the waitress for a second tall glass of lemonade. Sitting in the booth, Fr. Daniel thought through the precarious course of his priestly life the past year, how close he was to leaving. Oblivious to the people around him, he bowed his head and silently asked the Lord to restore his priesthood, to save the dozen years that he had given to Christ, to free him from the merciless guilt of his friend's death that inundated him.

"Excuse me, sir," the waitress said, looking at his handsome face, gently alerting the patron she thought asleep. "You finished here?"

"Yes," he muttered coming out of his prayer. "Yes, I am." She slipped the check onto the table and moved away. He placed some bills near it and slid out of the booth. The restaurant was full of people now. He felt a little paranoid, as if one of them might recognize him; he did not want to see anyone he knew.

As he sped down the highway, the radio twang with a bad, country version of one of his favorite songs, "Desperado," an old tune by the Eagles, that urged the listener to stop riding fences. He sighed at what he heard as an answer to his prayer. Driving he felt driven, pushed along by something larger than himself, an almost palpable hush enveloping him, compressing time, quieting the colors, sounds, and movements on the long ride through the West Virginia countryside. Then he saw a sign for Wheeling-Jesuit University. That's where we all met, he thought, remembering their carefree days at college together. He recalled the distinguished Fr. Desmond Pearce and their introductory class in the philosophy of God. He had heard that that venerable priest was back at the University, lecturing occasionally, helping where he could. *He must be seventy-five*, he thought. He glanced at his car clock: 6:35 p.m. The numbers glowed green and distinct on the dashboard panel. *Mass will be just about over and maybe he'll be hearing confessions like he used to,* Fr. Daniel thought. *It's been four or five months since I've been to confession.* He had been avoiding his spiritual director for the past few months as his ambivalence grew stronger. With the mission priest covering the vigil Mass at St. Anthony's he had the opportunity to stop at his alma mater. He took the exit for Wheeling-Jesuit and in a couple of minutes was turning off of Washington Street and onto the campus.

It had been quite a while since he had been on campus. This was the end of the semester: a few students were bustling across the grounds packing for home, while the rest were finishing papers or studying for final examinations. Fr. Daniel drove the length of the compact campus toward the Chapel of Mary and Joseph. He

parked his green LeSabre in the last lot. By the
time he neared the chapel, the vigil Mass was
letting out; he felt self-conscious being on campus without his clerical clothing. Passing the
middle-aged priest saying goodbye to the students as they left the chapel, he gave him a fraternal nod. Inside, he went to a pew near the
colorful icon of the Holy Family and waited
for the opportunity to make his confession.
What am I doing here? he thought, as perplexed
about how he ended up in this chapel at the
end of his day's wandering as he was about the
intricacies of the situation within which he was
ensnared. In a few minutes, the violet light
over the confessional blinked off, a penitent
came out and Fr. Daniel moved closer. He was
glad to have a few minutes to collect his
thoughts because time itself seemed to be racing this early evening, rising to some kind of
crescendo of stillness. When he finally got up
to take his turn he saw the name on the confes-

sional door: Fr. Desmond Pearce, S.J. He chose the privacy of the screen so his old professor would not recognize him.

"Bless me, Father, for I have sinned," Fr. Daniel whispered. "My last confession was around Christmas. I'm a priest."

"Excuse me, lad," Fr. Pearce said. "That last part; I couldn't hear you."

"I said I'm a Catholic priest," Fr. Daniel whispered closer to the screen.

"Oh," the old man said. "Thank you for gracing my confessional, Father."

"I don't know where to begin," Fr. Daniel said. "I've avoided my spiritual director for the past few months because I'm in crisis. I don't know if I can go on serving God."

"When did you stop praying, Father?" the old priest said.

The young priest knelt in stunned silence.

"Is there a woman?" The old priest straightened his back in the chair, hidden in the shadows of the confessional.

"Well, yes, but that's not it," Fr. Daniel said. "I mean we haven't been together, or anything like that."

"It's more than that, then?" Fr. Pearce said. "You think you love her?"

"I think so," the younger priest said squirming in his place. "Her husband and I were close friends since college, the three of us were. He and I went whitewater rafting on the Cheat River last year about this time and he drowned —I tried to save him but I couldn't." Beads of sweat formed on his forehead as he ground his teeth. "I feel like it's my fault he died and I have to make it up to his wife and kids."

"Noble, too, are you, Father?" the old priest said sarcastically. He was riveted to the voice of the younger man, drawn by its subtleties of shrewdness and delusion.

"What?" Fr. Daniel said.

"Was it an accident?" Fr. Pearce said.

"Yes; yes it was," the younger priest said.

"So, it's more than guilt driving you into her arms, lad?" Fr. Pearce said.

"Well, yes, I guess so," Fr. Daniel said and exhaled loudly. He felt like a tightly wound ball of string that was being unraveled.

"And does she love you?" the old priest said gently.

"I don't know," Fr. Daniel said. "I mean, it's only been a year since he died; she's still hurting. Her life's in disarray."

There was a pause in the parry of questions and answers. The old priest sat there waiting in the dark. An expectant hush filled the silence. Then something like a faint breeze quickened his frail, tired frame.

"What are you afraid of, Father?" the hidden priest said, striking out for the deep waters, unnerving the penitent. He had an intimation

that he was fighting for the young man's vocation, battling for his soul against that old enemy who was stalking him like some mountain
lion prowling the Appalachians for prey.

"I don't know," Fr. Daniel said, struck to
the quick by the insight of his question.

"It consumes you," Fr. Pearce countered.
"Death? Love? Mortality? Solitude? Commitment? God? What? What are you afraid of?"

The eloquent silence flayed the young man's
contorted conscience, opening his heart to the
tender hues of God's mercy. He began to cry.
"I'm afraid of a deeper life with God."

"So, you're afraid to draw closer to the
Lord," the old priest whispered, leaning toward
the screen. "That's why you stopped praying.
Because if you do draw closer to Him, there'll
be no turning back, no straddling the fence.
You're afraid to love God as He loves you,
aren't you, Father?"

"Yes," Fr. Daniel said, recognizing for the first time what had plagued his priesthood the past few years. He ran his hands through his thick head of black hair, pulling it taut.

"You won't give God what He wants," the old priest moved in like a skilled boxer throwing a relentless combination of punches. "He wants you without reservation, without holding back. You don't trust Him. The Lord wants to bless the work of your priestly hands."

"I'm frightened," Fr. Daniel said, the tears trickling down his face. "I'm at my wit's end and I'm frightened of God's love. I don't know Him very well."

"If you don't know him by now, you'll never know him, D—, Father," the old priest said, the long forgotten memory of the young man's voice almost giving rise to his name on Fr. Pearce's lips. The old priest was exhausted from the tension of battle, his eyes drooping, the sweat soaking his shirt. He felt his age like a cross on his back. He dozed a moment in the dark.

"Father Desmond," the young priest called out for him.

"Stay sober and alert, your enemy the devil is prowling like a roaring lion looking for someone to devour," the old priest muttered the verse from Peter that came to mind.

"What?" the young priest asked. "What did you say, Father?"

"God must have great work for you to do for the Evil One to conspire against you with such cunning. You're a priest forever, young man, according to the order of Melchizedek." The older man rallied for a moment in the dark, his spirit rising softly beneath the tired flesh, the blue eyes illumined by his soul gleaming in the purple shadows of the confessional. "You have to show your true colors, Father; you have to live out your vows to the Lord

God Almighty to whom you pledged your life. You must! Oh, and one more thing, young man. Where's the sin in all this?"

"The whole thing—I guess," Fr. Daniel said. "I don't know."

"Yes, you do, Father," the old priest said in his professorial tone so as not to let him off so easily. "Think."

"Jealousy? Guilt?" the young man offered. "Maybe I've been jealous of Ryan and Beth and their family all along."

"Maybe you coveted his wife and family because you should've been more deeply in love with God. We all have to love, Father: celibate, married, widowed," the old priest whispered. "But then you didn't pray about it; you didn't entrust your trouble to your heavenly Father. You didn't trust Him to love you despite your human weakness, or rather, because of it. You don't know much about God's mercy, do you lad?"

"I preach it every day." Fr. Daniel shook his head. "Yeah, you're right. I don't."

"Leave the woman alone," the old priest said deliberately. "You'll only prevent her from finding a good man to marry. Now, for your penance, read chapters 11 and 12 in the Second Book of Samuel." Fr. Pearce fumbled with the purple stole that lay across his lap. "It's the story of a man of God who covets another man's wife—d'you know it?"

"King David?" Fr. Daniel said.

"But the difference is you aren't responsible for your friend's death. You didn't have him killed to have his wife," the old priest spoke distinctly.

"Of course, yes," Fr. Daniel whispered, wiping his hand down his face.

"The Father of Lies has used your guilt to beguile you and confound your conscience with his half-truths and deceptions that nearly cost you your vocation. You invited him to pursue you when you stopped praying," the Jesuit father concluded, his body relaxing, now, the Spirit receding from the moment like a flame without oxygen. "Read Second Samuel and then go to the Cathedral where you were ordained and lay prostrate before the altar as you did years ago. Enter into deeper communion with Christ. He loves you very much, very much," the old priest's voice trailed off. He leaned his forehead against the screen between them. "More than you'll ever know."

Fr. Daniel prayed the Act of Contrition in one long breath.

The exhausted old priest could barely raise his arm for absolution, but he managed the words of forgiveness and the sign of the cross, in the recesses of the dark confessional where he had defeated the demons oppressing souls hundreds of times before.

"Thank you, Father," Fr. Daniel said into the purple blackness. "Thank you, Fr. Desmond."

"Peace be with you," Fr. Pearce said. "Pray for me, young man, that I might see God soon. Remember, the blessed Mother protects your vocation—it's May. Go to her; seek her intercession. She will protect you under her mantle. After all, you are one of her beloved sons, Father."

Fr. Daniel stepped out of the confessional and went to the bookrack in the narthex where he found a shelf of Bibles. He returned to his pew before the icon of the Holy Family and read the chapters from Samuel slowly, feeling the tension easing in his neck and shoulders. He prayerfully read about King David's murderous plot to have Uriah killed in battle so he could have Bathsheba for himself only to have Nathan the prophet expose his treachery. Finishing the chapters he began to feel extricated from the web of relationships within which he was entangled: free of the jealousy, free of the guilt, free. He prayed awhile, thanking God for that old priest who had saved his vocation. He stayed in the quiet chapel until the slow padding steps of Fr. Pearce faded beyond his hearing.

Fr. Daniel walked to his car in the cool, spring night. Within a few minutes, he was parking his LeSabre in front of St. Joseph Cathedral, the dusk light dull in the purple sky streaked with yellow haze. He knew that the side door off the courtyard would be opened now. The Cathedral shimmered in half-light; Mass had been over an hour ago. A lone janitor swept the narthex. Fr. Daniel took a few steps down the aisle. The pale light of dusk seemed to dull the bright reds, yellows, and blues of the murals and stained-glass windows; soft white lights lit the way down the center aisle. He genuflected as he approached the sanctuary, the majestic mural of Christ beckoning him with open arms. Fr. Daniel did what the old priest directed him to do: he lay prostrate before the altar of the Lord God Almighty in the same place as he had done a dozen years ago on the day of his ordination. He closed his eyes and could almost see the exquisite colors of grace like the aurora borealis spun into a single strand of light, as fine as thread, piercing his heart. "I love You, Lord. I'm sorry," he prayed, unafraid of that promised communion. "I love You." He rested his forehead on the back of his hands and a tear bathed the gold anchor painted on the floor tile beneath his face, washing away his sins, his fear and guilt, in that timeless sea of God's mercy as wide and fathomless as the passing millennium.

LAST PRIEST STANDING

"Has he been awake at all?" the tall young priest asked the nun in her modified veil and blue habit.

"In and out today," she answered. She held the old man's wrist and looked at her watch to check his pulse against the monitor.

"I'd like to anoint him, Sister." Fr. John raised his prayer book slightly. "He was my teacher in the seminary."

"Sure, Father," she said, laying the man's hand down on the bed. "The rector was here to anoint him last week after he fell down the stairs. It can't hurt."

"Has he had a lot of visitors?" Fr. John asked.

"More the last couple of days," she said. "I got to know him a little over the years. He was such a gentle, unassuming man. He must have been a great priest in his day—everyone has such wonderful things to say about him."

"He is a great priest," Fr. John said, staring intently at the serene and leathery face of his former seminary professor. "A holy man."

Fr. Duy Nguyen had been in this private room adjacent to the infirmary at the Motherhouse of the Daughters of Charity for more than a week now, having served the ill and aging nuns as chaplain for the past few years. He had lived here in Emmitsburg, Maryland, for the past forty years, ever since his escape from

Vietnam in 1975. When he was first placed in this pale, blue room after the accident, while his mind was still clear, he had a premonition that his life would come to an end here in this convent. And that was fine with him, as Emmitsburg had become his home. But, now, the morphine drip dangling beside the headboard of his bed eased the pain of his broken hip and sedated him so that the muted voices he heard mingled with the blurred memories and disjointed dreams rising in his intermittent consciousness.

"Father, do you know how he got that nasty scar on his leg?" Sister Grace Marie asked. "It looks like a big burn mark down the whole one side."

"Not really," Fr. John said. "I heard that he might have been in a fire years ago."

Fr. Nguyen's body seemed to twitch beneath the bedsheet and he exhaled loudly. Through his altered awareness over the past few days, he could sense time slipping away with each suppressed breath, like a clock ticking down toward the hour of his expiration. His one regret was that he would not recover the lost opportunities to do God's will, to celebrate the sacraments, to cooperate with that mysterious grace that always led him to do good and avoid evil. Time was the adversary now, formidable and final, winning as his life was being used up before their eyes in the inescapable death throes of a priest of God at the end of his earthly days. His dull prayer had now become not so much a dutiful petition open to the Creator, but rather the only intelligible language suitable for the numinous realm toward which his being was moving.

"Chú Duy?" a middle-aged Vietnamese couple in dark clothing asked as they stood in the doorway of his room.

"Yes," Fr. John said. "Fr. Nguyen."

The petite woman's dark eyes began to mist as they stepped closer to the dying priest's hospital bed.

"Chú was with us for many years," the man said.

"At Our Lady of Vietnam," his wife added.

They were from the small Vietnamese parish twenty miles west on the edge of a farming town in Western Maryland, where Fr. Nguyen had helped on the weekends while teaching at Mount Saint Mary Seminary.

"He's resting, now," Sister Grace said to them as she moved to the foot of the bed to make room for Fr. John to anoint him. "Father is going to pray. You can join us."

The couple smiled and nodded to her in appreciation.

Fr. John placed the thin, purple stole around his Roman collar to perform the priestly rite. "In the name of the Father," he began in a soft voice. "...and of the Son, and of the Holy Spirit."

Sister Grace and the couple made the sign of the cross on their bodies in sympathy with the words of blessing.

"Let this water call to mind our baptism into Christ who has redeemed us by his death and resurrection." Fr. John sprinkled holy water from a small plastic bottle across Fr. Nguyen's prone body, a few drops falling on his exposed arm and hand.

The sensation of the water on his skin coupled with the familiar words of prayer, gave rise in Chú Duy's distorted consciousness to the haunting memory of the desperate weeks that he and the other sixty refugees prayed fervently as they languished in their storm-tossed fishing boat in the South China Sea, with waves, at times, as tall as forest trees, the night sky black and ominous save the stars that were their only means of navigation, and the pirates

—the pirates who more than once raided their small craft for anything or, in the case of the younger women, anyone worth taking. He recalled them disembarking on the shores of Thailand and being led to the safety of a refugee camp bordering Malaysia, which would be their home for a couple of years. Then the relentless morphine washed away the recollection in a swirling wave of darkness.

Another visitor entered his room, an older Vietnamese man who nodded to the young priest and then stood silently next to the couple as Fr. John continued the abbreviated sacramental rite.

Quoting the biblical letter of the Apostle James, Fr. John read the verses aloud: "Are there sick among you? Let them send for the priests of the Church, and let the priests pray over them anointing them with oil in the name of the Lord..."

The woman began to sob, and her husband put his arm around her shoulder.

Then Fr. John set his prayer book down on the nightstand beside the bed. Silently, he reached over and placed his hands on Chú Duy's head with the ancient gesture of conferring blessing in the Judeo-Christian tradition. When he touched the crown of his frail professor's balding head, Fr. John had to restrain his tears.

The light press of Fr. John's warm hands upon Chú Duy's head caused the old priest to open his eyes, momentarily, to what he perceived as indistinct, shadowy figures, illumined by the afternoon light streaming through the lone window, with the vague outline of the crucifix looming above them on the wall opposite his bed. And then his swirling thoughts conjured that other time when the bishop laid his hands upon his head in the crowded cathedral the day of his ordination to the priesthood of Chúa Kitô. He remembered the proud faces of his father and mother that shining day, and then the morphine clouded his thoughts again.

Fr. John next took the small, cylindrical oil stock from the pocket of his black shirt, unscrewed the lid, and pushed his thumb onto the cotton ball that held the oils. Marking a small cross on Chú Duy's forehead with his oiled thumb, Fr. John prayed with reverence and feeling: "Through this holy anointing may the Lord in His love and mercy help you with the grace of the Holy Spirit."

Then, he gently turned Chú Duy's arm at the wrist and traced another cross on the palm of his hand, saying: "May the Lord who frees you from sin save you and raise you up."

He walked around the bed, past the others, to get to the priest's left hand, which was covered by the white bedsheet. Pulling the sheet down slightly, he saw Chú Duy's hand in a loose fist grasping a pair of rosary beads. He gently pried open the dying priest's fingers so that he could anoint this hand, too.

As soon as Fr. John touched the heel of his palm with his oiled thumb, Chú Duy's hand closed around the black beads, more a reaction of muscle memory than will. As the young priest brought the hem of the bedsheet up to his chest, again, Chú Duy's amorphous catalogue of memories brought to his veiled mind the pilgrimage Mass he had celebrated at the revered shrine of Our Lady of Lavang in Vietnam decades ago, when he had, what he could only describe later, as a mystical experience, during the penitential rite, of the mantle of the Blessed Virgin Mary wrapping around him, protectively. And ever since that mysterious day, this same pair of black rosary beads obtained at the shrine had remained in his hand or tucked away safely in his pocket for quick and easy access for public or private recitation.

"Now let us pray to God in the words the Lord Jesus taught us," Fr. John said and leaned down near to Chú Duy's ear. "Our Father..."

As he and Sister Grace prayed the Lord's Prayer in English, the three Vietnamese visitors raised their voices in the mellifluous tones of their fluid, oriental tongue: "*Lạy Cha chúng con ở trên trời, chúng con nguyện danh Cha cả sáng, nước Cha trị đến, ý Cha thể hiện dưới đất cũng như trên trời.*"

Fr. John's close voice, and the melodic murmuring of his former parishioners in his native language, stirred Chú Duy; and he imperceptibly tried to move his lips in synchronization with their prayer. Then, like a nightmare, the ferocious image of a scowling demon emerged out of the blackness of his drugged mind to threaten the guilt-ridden priest one last time, taunting him with flames rising from his claws, prompting Chú Duy to dreadfully recall that ruinous fire he had caused twenty-five years

329

ago in the rectory of Our Lady of Vietnam while the pastor was away: falling asleep with a bourbon in one hand and a lit cigarette in the other, until, awaking from his stupor, the flames had already engulfed the living room curtains, licking up the walls, before he realized that his pant leg was burning, too, and it was all he could do to pat out the fire on his clothing and, coughing from the smoke, stumble out of the burning rectory to call for help from the church. Even in his sedation, Chú Duy could still feel the guilt from his careless negligence that had brought such shame to him and the parish. For the next fifteen years, as payment for the damage he had caused, he would not cash nor deposit any of the honorarium or stipend checks that he received from the parish. He had never forgiven himself for that destructive fire, nor for his self-pity when he lost track of his younger brother and sister in Vietnam after their parents had died and he took to a habit of indulgent and excessive drinking for a few years in the decade of the nineteen-nineties. Though Chúa had long forgiven him, Satan had not forgotten.

Sister Grace noticed the spike in his blood pressure and heartbeat on the monitor as they continued to pray.

"*Xin Cha cho chúng con hôm nay lương thực hằng ngày, và tha nợ chúng con như chúng con cũng tha kẻ có nợ chúng con. Xin chớ để chúng con sa chước cám dỗ, nhưng cứu chúng con cho khỏi sự dữ. Amen,*" they completed the Lord's Prayer, the Vietnamese a little ahead of the priest and sister.

Returning to the other side of the bed, Fr. John picked up his prayer book to finish the rite of anointing. He prayed the closing prayer for a soul near death, and again the woman's soft sobs punctuated his words. Then the young priest raised his right hand for the final blessing. "May God the Father bless you. May

God the Son heal you. May God the Holy Spirit enlighten you," he said.

The familiar words of blessing moved Chú Duy to instinctively try to raise his right hand to join the priestly gesture, but the impulse only caused his fingers to twitch so slightly that the others did not even notice.

"May almighty God bless you." Fr. John made the sign of the cross over him. "The Father, and the Son, and the Holy Spirit. Amen."

"Amen," they all responded.

Then everyone was quiet. Fr. John put the lid on the oil stock and slipped it into his shirt pocket. He did the same with the bottle of holy water. He took the purple stole from around his neck, kissed it at the embroidered gold cross, folded it neatly and laid it atop his prayer book on the nightstand.

"Thank you, Father," Sister Grace said. "You said he was your teacher—he must've meant a lot to you."

"He does," Fr. John said. "He was the Mariology professor at the Mount for a generation of priests," he explained. "He helped make my devotion to Mary a real part of my faith. One time I concelebrated Mass with him for thousands of Vietnamese people who came on a pilgrimage to the Our Lady of Lourdes Grotto on the top of the hill. I don't speak a word of Vietnamese, but he needed help with communion, so I helped."

Another younger priest in Roman collar came into the room.

Fr. John moved to greet him and the two shook hands near the doorway, away from the bed.

"Mike, I just anointed him," Fr. John said. "He's fading."

"Good to see you, John," Fr. Michael said. "It's been a while."

"At the convocation in Baltimore last year," Fr. John said.

"I was hoping to take one last trip with him to Gettysburg this summer," Fr. Michael said. "Did you ever go with him to the battlefield?"

"Just once," Fr. John said. "A couple years after we were ordained, a few of us went with him for a day trip."

"He knew as much as the park guides," Fr. Michael said, trying to lower his voice. "As soon as we'd cross the Mason-Dixon Line into Pennsylvania, he'd begin to recount the days of the battle like he had been there or something."

"Yeah, I remember," Fr. John said and glanced fondly at their teacher.

"I think they even let him guest lecture in the college history class a few times," Fr. Michael whispered. "Gettysburg was like his hobby."

The Vietnamese couple and the older man stood quietly at the foot of Chú Duy's bed. Sister Grace glanced at the animated priests as she left the room to attend to other patients in the infirmary.

The reminiscent whispers of his former students brought to Chú Duy's mind the surreal memory of his escape from Vietnam with his friend and colleague. In a final burst of clarity, in spite of his muddled mind, he once again heard the last instructions of their hopeful bishop that night and his admonition taken from St. Paul: "Even if your heart convicts you, Christ is stronger than your heart." With the forced closing of the seminary, they came to understand what their wise bishop already knew: that, if they did make it, they would be overwhelmed with guilt later in their lives for what might seem to have been the abandonment of their family, friends, country, and church. The shrewd bishop had also known that the noose was tightening around their necks, and it would not be long before the communist authorities would arrest his young, learned professors and eventually grind their lives to dust in a prison camp or brutally kill them as they had done to dozens of his good priests since the end of the war. Chú Duy recalled the perilous journey through the jungle and along footpaths for several days trying to avoid people and villages until they reached the Mekong River with the soldiers on their trail only a couple of hours behind them. He remembered resting awhile and praying together before they began to paddle and kick their way across that wide, treacherous water on their small, crude rafts made of coconuts bound with strands of fiber stripped from palm trees to buoy them. Despite the morphine haze that dissipated his memory, he lived through the horrors of that nightmare again: the numbing cold of the night river, the random gunfire, the patrol boats and spotlights searching the dark waters, the dangerous tree limbs bobbing past them in the swift current, and then, as he awoke from an exhausted doze, his companion's terrified gasp as he was dragged down into the murky river by something large enough to swallow a man's leg. With all the strength of will that he could muster against the narcotic's insistence, Chú Duy recalled his desperate appeal to the Blessed Mother for deliverance in that unbroken rosary that he prayed until the dawn. Exhausted to the point of death, hungry and hopeless, he remembered waking to feel his hand touching the sandy bank on the other side of the morning delta. Chú Duy recalled his first, joyful steps on that riverbank in Cambodia, until the morphine eased him ever closer to his inevitable and ultimate destination.

Sister Grace Marie returned to the room to check on her patient. The young priests were still whispering cherished stories about their beloved teacher. Fr. Nguyen's former parishioners were kneeling at the foot of his bed finishing the rosary in Vietnamese. Sister Grace kissed the hand of the dying priest and her tear bathed his wrist.

"He'll rest now," she said to the others and fussed with the bedsheet at his chest. "It won't be long now. I'll stay with him."